THE EDGE OF DISASTER

Edwina flung Mrs. Clemens roughly over onto her back and probed at her throat for a pulse: nothing. Tipping the head back, Edwina blew two quick puffs of air down her windpipe and listened at her chest. No breathing.

Edwina ripped the woman's housedress unceremoniously open. Kneeling, she laced her fingers one hand atop the other, pressing the heel of the lower one to the woman's flaccid chest. But, as she did, she heard a thundering sound that flung her reflexively face-down across the woman's body. A rumble shuddered through the earth. Edwina jumped up and was abruptly knocked flat by the blast.

By the time she got her wits back enough to know which end of herself was pointed up, she saw Mrs. Clemens's lifeless body just a few feet away. *Airway, breathing, pulse,* Edwina thought, feeling her own limbs moving zombielike toward the victim.

Rough hands caught her from behind and turned her. A man's anxious face peered into her own...

St. Martin's Paperbacks Titles
by Mary Kittredge

FATAL DIAGNOSIS
RIGOR MORTIS
CADAVER *(coming in 1993)*

RIGOR MORTIS

MARY KITTREDGE

ST. MARTIN'S PAPERBACKS

RIGOR MORTIS

Copyright © 1991 by Mary Kittredge.

Library of Congress Catalog Card Number: 90-49295

ISBN: 0-312-92865-3

Printed in the United States of America

St. Martin's Press hardcover edition/February 1991
St. Martin's Paperbacks edition/October 1992

10 9 8 7 6 5 4 3 2 1

ONE

MILLIE Clemens nearly screamed when she saw Hiram Greenspan coming at her with the hypodermic.

"No," she quavered. "I'm not taking it. You put that thing away."

Hiram Greenspan looked puzzledly at the syringe in his hand. It was filled with a clear, pale yellow solution of vitamins, minerals, and trace elements mixed in sterile normal saline.

"Millie, there's nothing here to be afraid of." He bounced the apparatus lightly on his palm, as if to demonstrate its harmlessness. "I've been giving you this stuff for years, so why don't you just turn around now and we'll—"

"You take one single step nearer to me with that thing," said the elderly woman perched on the edge of Hiram's examining table, "and I'll stick it in you and shoot *you* full of poison. And we'll just see how you like *that*."

Sadly, Hiram recapped the needle he had been about to plunge into this silly old bat's wrinkled buttock. He knew it was wrinkled because he'd seen it a hundred times before, and he knew she was a silly old bat because she'd said what she'd just said.

And that was what made Hiram Greenspan feel suddenly so bad. Millie, he thought, why did you have to go and lose your marbles on me after all this time? Couldn't you wait a little longer, at least until I'd retired?

"How long has it been, now, Millie?" Hiram asked. "Since Walter died, I mean."

Because that was what had knocked her off balance, he felt sure, Walt Clemens up and dying so suddenly as he had. Hiram had seen that before, too: an old married couple hitched together all those years, they were like a pair of matched plow horses. You take one away, the other one couldn't pull straight anymore.

Hiram dropped the loaded syringe into the discarded sharps box on the counter by the sink. Then, because he couldn't quite think of anything else to do, he began to wash his hands.

"Sixteen days, twelve hours, and twenty minutes," Millie replied finally.

Hiram looked down at the thick, white, antiseptic lather he was building from his forearms to his fingertips. He had always liked Millie. Walt too, of course, although not quite so much. Angrily he made the running water hotter.

"Getting any sleep at all, are you?"

She made an exasperated noise with her lips. He figured it meant no. From the other sounds he knew too that she had climbed down off the examining table and was pulling on her clothes.

Hiram concentrated on cleaning his fingernails with one of the green-and-white disposable nailbrushes the detail man from the pharmaceutical company had been handing out the last time he came around with his briefcase full of miracle drugs for everything from asthma to zonulitis. Green and white were the hallmark colors of the pharmaceutical company the detail man worked for.

Hiram thought the nailbrushes were pretty good, although he didn't think much of the miracle drugs. In his experience the more miracles any drug promised, the more rotten and potentially dangerous side effects it would probably deliver, too.

Then the detail man would try to sell you on a new drug to take care of all the problems caused by the old one, and after that a third drug to mop up the damage from the second—none of which you would have had to worry about in the first place if you'd just smiled and taken the free nailbrushes and tossed the detail man out of your office on his backside.

Which was what Hiram had done. Now he worked on his nails with the disposable nailbrush, out of habit and to give his patient time to finish getting her dress zipped before he turned around.

When he had dried his hands and faced her, though, she had not gotten it zipped. She just stood there weeping with her hands, liver-spotted and arthritic, hanging at her sides.

"I'm sorry I spoke to you that way," she managed. "But you don't believe me either, do you, Hiram? No one does. They just think I'm a stupid old woman."

Hiram sighed and made a circling motion, index finger aimed down. Millie turned, obedient as a child, and let him zip her up the back. As bad as her arthritis was lately, he couldn't imagine how she managed it alone, but he supposed women had their ways.

Not that he would ever know, he thought with a

brief burst of bitterness at himself. The dress had a tiny hook and loop atop the zipper; there were no such things on men's clothes and he fumbled it a bit before managing to get it secured.

"I don't think you're stupid, Millie," he said.

He was glad she hadn't said senile, though. He didn't know what he would have answered if she had; Hiram Greenspan would no more lie to a patient than he would do with one what he was thinking of doing with Millie now.

"There you go," he said gently, giving the zipper a final, unnecessary little tug. "Now go splash your face, and then come on down to the consulting room."

Millie nodded without turning back to him. He knew she did not want him to see her tears again, which from the movements of her shoulders were still flowing steadily and silently.

Poor old Millie, he thought, leaving the examining room and closing the door quietly behind him; she had been a beautiful woman once.

In fact to Hiram she still was a beautiful woman, and if she had not been quite so recent a widow he might have done what he was thinking of doing instead of patting her on the shoulder and walking away. At least he might have invited her to dinner in a restaurant, and if she ever got her emotional keel leveled out again, there was still a halfway decent chance of that.

But now there was this damned irrational outburst of hers to consider. Paranoid was how she seemed, not only refusing the vitamins but, earlier, ordering his office nurse out of the examining room. Mrs. Williston had seemed quite insulted when she told him about it, and had stalked straight away to work off her temper in a fit of file-drawer reorganizing.

4

Shaking his head as he sank into the big old leather chair behind his desk, Hiram supposed Millie must have said something dreadful to his old nurse—which was odd all by itself, since Millie had known and liked Mrs. Williston for years.

And then there was Millie's drinking. He'd had it out with her before about that, and maybe he would have to again. It wasn't a chronic thing, but she did tend to hit the bottle now and then when she needed a painkiller.

Which she did now, he thought. Quite reasonably, too, and Hiram intended to give her one. At the sound of her shoes coming down the hall, he straightened.

No booze. Vitamin pills, since she wouldn't take the shots. And something for her sleep, something simple and effective so she wouldn't sit up all night emptying the liquor cabinet.

If she didn't straighten out pretty quick on that regime, he would have to start believing that her trouble might be worse than simple grief, especially if the outbursts and suspiciousness continued.

People sometimes developed such symptoms to cover the early confusion of Alzheimer's disease. And for them you had to start thinking right away about what would happen later: about how and where they would get the long-term care they would be needing when the awful day came that they could no longer remember how to comb their hair, how to use a bathroom or dress themselves or get food into their mouths. Hiram was hoping he wouldn't end up having to arrange that sort of care for Millie Clemens when the door to his consulting room opened and she came in.

"I've apologized to Mrs. Williston," she said. "I'm

5

sorry I made such a fuss." She took a hanky from her purse and dabbed at her large, pale grey eyes.

"It's just that she did fiddle with Walter's intravenous. The nurse at the hospital, I mean, not Mrs. Williston, of course, and then Walter died." She snapped the hanky back into her purse.

"The way it all happened," she went on, "one thing after the other so fast, it didn't seem right no matter what they said about not finding anything at Walter's . . . at his . . ."

"Postmortem examination," Hiram supplied. The phrase seemed somehow more tactful than the blunt word *autopsy*.

And as Millie said, nothing strange had been found at it. The old boy had simply popped off— boom—of cardiac arrest while recuperating— poorly—from gallbladder surgery.

Considering Walt's age and his general physical condition, which Hiram Greenspan characterized privately as piss-poor, this was not a bit mysterious. That he'd died just seconds after his night nurse turned up the flow rate on his IV tubing was just plain bad luck, especially for the nurse who had gotten a fairly serious grilling on account of Millie's yelling murder.

Which she was still yelling now, and Hiram Greenspan did not know how to make her stop. The only thing he could think of was to try to get her a few nights' unbroken sleep, in hopes it might start her along on some sort of natural healing process.

There were risks to that approach too, he realized; miracle drugs were not the only ones with side effects.

"You wouldn't abuse medication I ordered for you, would you, Millie? You'd take it strictly according to my instructions."

Millie Clemens tightened her lips and glared at him. "Stop treating me like a fool, Hiram."

Then stop acting like one, he thought, but of course he did not say this as he took out a prescription pad and wrote on it.

"Don't take it with alcohol," he warned, handing the slip of paper to her and making a mental note to see her next week; if she needed the tough lecture, he would give it to her then.

"And don't plan on staying up afterwards," he added. "Just swallow it and get right into bed. It works fast."

Like a ton of bricks, he might have said, but he figured she could find that out for herself.

Frowning, she accepted the prescription. "I guess I might as well try it."

"Good." He nodded approvingly, beginning to feel a bit more hopeful about that restaurant invitation. "Here's one for some multivitamins, too. Maybe by next time we'll get you back on the injections."

Millie looked at him sharply but did not comment. He wasn't sure the vitamin shots did any good, but she'd perked up so much when he'd started her on them years ago that he was unwilling now to perform the experiment of stopping them.

"And Millie," Hiram said, "try to . . ." He hesitated, unsure how to say it.

Biting her lip, Millie gazed down at the prescription slips. She had been his patient now for nearly thirty years. "I know, Hiram," she said. "I'll try, I really will. And . . . thank you."

Then with a sad little smile she walked out of his office, leaving him to wonder if he had done everything he could for her.

Vitamins and chloral hydrate: maybe they would

do the trick, but somehow at the moment they simply did not seem like enough. Probably the detail man had some miracle remedy in his briefcase, some wonder drug guaranteed to banish the fears and pains, the awful loneliness of old age.

Or maybe he should have just put his arms around her, after all.

* * *

"No," said Mrs. Bernier Crosley-White, tenting her brittle old fingers and pursing her lips as she pondered Edwina Crusoe's question, "I don't think I need a sleeping pill tonight, dear."

Mrs. Crosley-White smiled sweetly at Edwina, showing off her full set of perfect teeth. At eighty-five she was proud of still possessing these, as she was of the rest of her very remarkable appearance: silver curls, bright blue eyes, cheeks round and pink as winter apples. In addition, her personality combined the seasoned shrewdness of long experience with an ingrained tendency to optimism.

As a result Mrs. Crosley-White was inclined to prepare for the worst while looking forward to the best, a habit Edwina found refreshing in persons of any age.

"In fact now that you are here," said this elderly paragon, "I am sure I shall have no difficulties whatsoever." And as if to prove it she settled back in bed, folding her hands across the bodice of her flowered flannel nightdress.

"Old ladies like me don't need much sleep," she confided as her eyelids fell shut like suddenly lowered crepe-silk draperies, "but I shall rest. Yes, I shall do that now, I think."

Moments later Mrs. Crosley-White was snoring softly. Edwina checked the volutrol on the IV, making a mental note to refill it at four A.M., and snapped off the light behind Mrs. Crosley-White's bed. In the glow of the small reading lamp by her own chair, the hospital room seemed suddenly cozy, safe, and comfortable.

We will have a quiet night, Edwina thought, looking forward with some gratification to the silent hours ahead. From the window whose venetian blinds Mrs. Crosley-White had requested not be closed, she could see New Haven all glittering with lights, the turnpike like an iridescent ribbon running through it.

One whole wing of the hospital jutted to her left, its rows and rows of windows making it resemble an enormous ship set sail upon an ocean of sky, while to her right spread the waters of the actual harbor, now an inky patch of deepest black broken only by the winking of the channel buoys, and at the docks by the glare of the deck lamps on tanker and container vessels.

On the windowsill crowded the silver-framed photographs of Mrs. Crosley-White's many children and grandchildren; among these a space had been cleared for Edwina's own things: two bottles of SoHo brand natural ginseng soda, a tuna fish and alfalfa sprouts sandwich on black bread, and a book entitled *Practical Homicide Investigation: Tactics, Procedures, and Forensic Techniques*.

In deference to Mrs. Crosley-White's reasons for asking her here, however, Edwina had taken the precaution of replacing this book's dust jacket with one from a different book: *The Shell Seekers*, by Rosamunde Pilcher.

Edwina thought this too was an excellent volume, remarkably well-plotted and beautifully written in addition to being quite gorgeously produced, only perhaps not of quite such immediately practical usefulness as Vernon J. Geberth's treatise on the finding and capturing of murderers.

The only trouble with the Geberth book lay in the pictures, which really were rather ghastly. But Geberth's was a textbook, not a romance novel, and one could hardly expect murder victims to lie down in attitudes of pleasant repose merely to spare the sensibilities of those privileged not to share their fate.

Opening a bottle of ginseng soda, a beverage Edwina found eminently restorative—in fact the stuff had a kick like a Kentucky mule—Edwina turned to Geberth's chapter on the first police officer's duties upon arriving at a murder scene.

These, it turned out, included (1) determining whether the victim was alive or dead, and whether or not to call for medical assistance; (2) apprehending the perpetrator or giving notice to other officers if escaped; and (3) keeping crime-scene evidence from contamination while detaining any witnesses and/or suspects.

All this sounded to Edwina like quite some trick, especially since the officer was also expected to identify and detain suspects, keep a chronological log of persons entering the crime scene—clergy, medical examiner, supervisors, other officers, and so on— and separate the witnesses so as to get independent statements from them.

Intelligently, however, Vernon J. Geberth had developed an acronym, one word that if kept in mind would help the officer on a murder scene remember all the things he or she was expected to do. The acronym was ADAPT: Arrest the perpetrator if possible, Detain witnesses and suspects, Assess the crime scene and Protect it, and perhaps most important of all, Take notes.

How absolutely ingenious, Edwina thought, paging swiftly past the photograph of a man who was looking somewhat the worse for wear. This Edwina found understandable, since the man had been hit on the head with some sharp nonyielding object, probably a spade or a pickaxe, and then tossed into a body of nonsterile water where he had floated about rather aimlessly for over a week before being discovered and fished out, whereupon his own body had been referred to the medical examiner.

In her bed Mrs. Crosley-White shifted and sighed. Marking her place, Edwina looked up. Her patient now resembled an elderly lady, soundly and peacefully asleep, which was precisely what she was supposed to resemble. Also, she no more needed a private-duty nurse than a flying fish needed water wings.

Still Mrs. Crosley-White had wanted company: skilled, well-experienced company of the sort who could prevent her from being stealthily murdered in her bed, an event she greatly feared after two other elderly patients had died unexpectedly in the night during the previous week.

This fear, of course, was entirely unfounded and might more cheaply have been dispelled by the abandonment of thrillers, a type of literature to which the good lady was addicted. But she could not be persuaded to give them up; meanwhile, she had for years been bosom friends' with Harriet Crusoe, who was among other things Edwina Crusoe's mother. Thus Edwina had been mustered into night-nurse duty, this service being rendered with the clear understanding that it was for one night only.

The duty, however, was proving unexpectedly congenial. From the dimly lit corridor came the low rumble of the medication cart being wheeled from room to room, the muted voice of the overhead page operator, and the squeaking of ripple-soled Nursemate shoes. From the corridor too came the smell of coffee brewing, a perfume that brought back memories of other night shifts when instead of caring for one patient Edwina had been in charge of two dozen.

The aroma persuaded her to abandon her ginseng soda in favor of the potion burbling in the nursing-station percolator, and she had just laid down her book with the idea of going to investigate this possibility when a woman down the corridor began screaming.

At the sound Mrs. Crosley-White sat up in bed. She was not the sort of woman to say "I told you so," but this phrase was the one her blue eyes expressed most clearly as she turned them upon Edwina.

"Why don't you go and find out what all the fuss is, dear?" she said.

* * *

The medication cart had been shoved aside to make room for the portable EKG machine, a defibrillator, and the code cart whose top was covered now with a brace of large glass ampules and a clutter of other instruments.

Inside the room the overhead lights glared whitely onto a bed from which linens were thrown back; through the doorway Edwina glimpsed a pair of hands fastening EKG leads onto a pair of pale white ankles.

"Vee-fib," said someone in the room, "better grease those paddles."

There was the popping sound of an electrical spark; the ankles jerked feebly and were still again.

"Rats," somebody else said, "straight-line. What the hell happened here, does anybody know?"

"You killed her," whispered a small pale woman standing in the corridor. Edwina turned to look at the young woman, who was wearing a navy knit dress, beige stockings, and low-heeled leather shoes. She had short yellow hair, fine features, and a general look of being accustomed to getting what she wanted, pronto. In both hands she clutched a brown leather handbag whose handle she worked convulsively between her fingers.

"I saw you," the woman whispered, her accusing stare aimed at a frightened-looking nurse who stood alone by the medication cart.

"No," the nurse said softly, glancing about as if searching for some route of escape. Her knuckles whitened on the edge of the cart.

"Twelve-thirty-four A.M.," said someone in the room.

"No," the nurse said again. She was about twenty-five years old, wearing a uniform dress, white stockings, and moccasin-style white nursing shoes; pinned to the breast pocket of her dress was a name tag that read Jillian Nash, RN.

The resuscitation team began filing from the room, interns and residents looking resentful since if they were not going to get any sleep they would have liked at least to save someone.

Realizing what had happened, the woman dropped her purse. "You *killed* her," she shrieked, rushing at the nurse by the medication cart. "You *gave* her something, I *saw* you!"

Edwina saw both of the young woman's hands very clearly. They were entirely empty. Next, before anyone could stop her, she had plunged them both into the stunned and unresisting nurse's skirt pockets. Pulling them out again, she waved a small glass vial in the left one.

"I saw you put this in your pocket," she insisted, "and I want to know what it is, I want it analyzed—*and* whatever she threw away in there, into the wastebasket."

The nurse now resembled a rabbit caught in the headlights of an oncoming eighteen-wheeler. Meanwhile, the rest of the gathered staff seemed suddenly to come to life again.

"Miss Bennington," said the charge nurse, "why don't you come and sit with the chaplain, here? Naturally you're upset, but I'm sure you don't mean—"

The chaplain was at that moment exiting the room, where he had gone to give a final blessing. In his wake two nurse's aides went in with what Edwina recognized as a wrapped shroud kit, while another began gathering the loops of EKG paper littering the floor.

"I do mean it," snapped the woman in the navy dress, "and I don't want any chaplain. I want the police, and I want them here right this minute."

The accused nurse flattened against the wall as if praying she could vanish through it.

"Excuse me," said Edwina, stepped forward.

Everyone knew her; she had worked at Chelsea Memorial Hospital for fifteen years before taking up her present occupation of private nurse-consultant. Now they all looked at her as if she might offer some quick cure for this most unpleasant situation.

But a quick cure was beyond her ability to provide; all one could hope for here, she thought, was to adapt. "I wonder," she said, "if perhaps we ought to call the nursing supervisor? She should be the one to notify the police. As," she added with deliberate understatement, "there does seem to be some problem, and it might as well be handled according to protocol."

Nodding, the charge nurse went off at once to do this.

"Also," Edwina said to the aides now working in the room, "you needn't trouble to disturb any catheters or tubings. And do not bathe the patient, please. Simply wrap the body loosely as it is, and don't discard anything, not even the EKG tapes. And don't let housekeeping in there—leave the room uncleaned."

She turned to the nurse who had been charting on the attempt at resuscitation. "You might want to list names of everyone who went in since the emergency began," she suggested quietly, "and add a brief note on the events out here as you observed them."

"I was going to write a note anyway," the nurse replied, and Edwina smiled at her. People who understood their business were always such a pleasure.

"Fine," she said. "Now about the vial, Mrs. Bennington—"

The accusing woman looked defiant. "Miss Bennington," she corrected. "And I'm keeping it until the police get here," she said. "Who knows what you people might do with it, if—"

"Yes, I do see your point." Edwina pressed her fingertips together consideringly. "But you see, if this situation should go any further—"

"Oh, it will," Miss Bennington stated grimly, "I guarantee you that." She shot a glare at the frightened-looking nurse.

"Indeed," said Edwina. "Well, then. I'm sure you wouldn't want there to be a question of what you had done with it. Not that I think you would do anything, of course, but evidence ought to be properly secured. Don't you agree?"

The woman in the navy dress looked doubtful. It was not an expression that agreed with her. "I suppose, but—"

"Perhaps," Edwina went on smoothly, "if I were to seal it in an envelope of yours. I see you have a packet of stationery in your handbag."

The handbag had fallen open upon dropping to the floor, and several sheets of letterhead stationery had slipped from it.

"An envelope of yours, locked in the narcotics cabinet at the nursing station," Edwina went on, "should keep it securely until it is wanted, I think."

"All right," the woman agreed grudgingly. Then she opened her mouth to say something unpleasant to the frightened nurse.

"Good," said Edwina, stepping quickly between them, "let's do that at once, then. We'll need the charge nurse, and the chaplain can come along, too, and you'll all watch me as I do it. May I have the vial, Miss Bennington?"

Reluctantly, the young woman handed it over: a tiny glass bottle with a sealed-on rubber stopper through which a hypodermic needle could be inserted to draw out the contents. A few drops of clear fluid remained at the bottom of it. But it was the vial's label that interested Edwina most, and when she read it she looked again at the nurse from whose pocket it had been extracted.

"Perhaps you'd better come along, too, Miss Nash," she said, "and wait in the charge nurse's office for the police to arrive."

*　*　*

"Morning," said Mrs. Crosley-White wonderingly. "It always seems like such a miracle to me."

Edwina looked up from her book, which lay open but unread in her lap. The room's square of window was filling with pale grey light, diluting the glow of the reading lamp. Reaching back she snapped it off.

"Shall I bring you a basin?" she asked, rising, "and get you your soap and tooth things?"

"Oh, no, dear. We mustn't leave the day nurse with nothing to do. But I would like a nice cup of tea, very strong and hot."

Her face eager as a child's, Mrs. Crosley-White turned back to the window to finish appreciating the dawn of another day. Surely, Edwina thought, there is a lesson here, but at the moment she felt too troubled to pick out what it was.

After sealing the suspect medication vial into one of Miss Bennington's stationery envelopes and locking the envelope in the narcotics cabinet, she had returned to the nursing station to find the night-shift nursing supervisor there.

With the supervisor were a pair of police officers, neither of whom was apparently quite sure what to do. As soon as she spotted them, however, Miss Bennington had begun informing them loudly and in no uncertain terms of what their duties were.

"I want her arrested," Miss Bennington snapped, "for murder. And I want it done now."

One of the policemen asked if Miss Bennington didn't think a hospital inquiry would suffice, as this would lead to charges if any turned out to be warranted.

"If?" she replied incredulously. "She put something in my aunt's intravenous, slipped something else into her pocket and left the room, and now my aunt is dead. I don't quite see what more *inquiry*," she pronounced it venomously, "could be required."

The policemen frowned. "What do you say about that, Miss Nash?" But the nurse sitting pale and shaken at the desk only shook her head, eyes downcast at her clasped hands.

"You must have some explanation," the nursing supervisor urged. "This is very serious, you know. If you've made an error in your medications, you'd better say so."

Jillian Nash looked up. "I don't know what happened," she said softly, her gaze dropping back to her hands again.

"Ask her," Miss Bennington challenged, "about the others. The other patients," she amplified, "who've died here unexpectedly this week. *Both* on the night shift, I heard, and both of them suddenly. I'll bet," she added in tones full of spite, "*she* was on duty both times."

She crossed her arms, tapping her foot impatiently. "Well, why don't you ask her about it?"

Jillian Nash straightened. "You don't have to ask me," she replied in a voice barely audible, "anyone can tell you I was here. You can check it on the time sheet. I was passing medications both nights—that's been my assignment all week."

The faces of the policemen grew severe. One was a big ruddy Irishman, the other lean, dark, and somewhat sly-appearing. "You took care of two other victims?" asked the bigger man.

"Yes," Jillian Nash said too quickly for Edwina to object. "But they weren't victims, not the way you mean. They died," she emphasized, "of natural causes."

"And this vial that was just now found in your possession, what was that?"

"Pancuronium," she answered. "It keeps you from moving, or even breathing. I don't know how it got in my pocket. None of my patients are receiving it. And I didn't give anything wrong to Miss Bennington's aunt. Or to any other patients, either," she finished defiantly.

Edwina frowned; Jillian Nash was getting her wind back and using it to make unwary statements, ones she seemed to think would get her out of the trouble she was in.

"You know," she told Jillian, "you face considerable legal jeopardy, here. You ought to take advice before you speak."

The nursing supervisor looked nonplussed as if realizing belatedly her duty toward Jillian Nash. "Miss Crusoe is right," she said. "I'm going to call the director of nursing. She'll get in touch with hospital counsel. But that," she added gently to the accused nurse, "may not help you, you realize."

Jillian Nash nodded. She was frightened but not stupid, understanding that if the hospital could defend itself by throwing her overboard it would do so in an instant. Every staff nurse knew it; it was simply the way things were.

"Am I under arrest?" she asked, her voice still soft but now surprisingly steely. It was as if she had thought all along it would come to this.

The ruddy-faced officer, clearly lead partner of the team, looked helplessly about. Dead patients, confiscated medicine bottles, and wild, unsubstantiated—

one hoped they were unsubstantiated—claims of murder. What in the world was a tired old beat cop to do?

"You'd better come with us," he told Jillian at last, "and answer a few more questions. After," he added with a cautious look toward Edwina, "I read to you about your rights."

And that had been that. Jillian Nash had been taken away, along with the vial in the envelope. The night shift had gone on without further event, other nurses doubling up on their assignments so Jill's could be covered.

Young Miss Bennington too had departed from the ward, while her aunt's body was wheeled down to the morgue to await the attentions of a pathologist.

And Mrs. Crosley-White had woken unmurdered, delighted at another morning. Edwina set the tea on her bedside table. From the radio a Mozart string quartet sprang undaunted into the room.

"Such a sense of humor," Mrs. Crosley-White murmured. "He was terribly ill when he wrote this, you know. Laughing in the face of death." She opened her eyes. "So heartening, Mozart's good example. Thank you for the tea, dear."

"You're welcome," said Edwina, distracted but not wanting to seem so.

The old lady sipped her hot beverage, enjoying it. "I shall be going home today, you know."

"Yes," said Edwina, wondering among other things why Jillian Nash would put a bottle of deadly stuff into her uniform pocket.

Mrs. Crosley-White put down her teacup. "It is a great relief to me. I knew the others were murdered, you see, although it didn't do to say so except to your mother. No one ever believes old ladies but other equally old ladies, I have found."

"Please," said Edwina, "think of me as an exception."

"Yes, quite," said Mrs. Crosley-White. She smiled, then got back to the point.

"They take us to the sun-room on bright days, you know. So kind of the staff. It's difficult staying in bed when one is used to being active. I go in a wheelchair—this bunion business is a bother—but Mr. Milton always made the trip leaning on a pair of canes. It's true he was elderly and so was Mrs. Freeman, so no one was terribly surprised when they passed away, but—"

"Except for you," said Edwina. "You were surprised."

"Indeed. After all, I'd nothing to do but to observe, had I? Mr. Milton was not by any means a dying man, Edwina, and as for Mrs. Freeman— why, she was positively peppy. Within the limits of her frailties, of course," the old lady added.

She shook her silver head. "Now they are gone, and last night another one, and it seems this young nurse supposedly has done it. So sad, but worrisome as well, don't you agree?"

Turning, she fixed upon Edwina the bright, unfooled eyes of the inveterate thriller-reader. "Since," she added, "I really cannot help wondering . . ."

"Why?" Edwina finished for her. "What reason could Jillian Nash have had for killing patients?"

"Just so," said the old lady, gratified. "My dear, you have put your finger on it."

*　　*　　*

There, thought Millie Clemens, licking the envelope flap and pounding it shut with her fist. The thump made her wrist ache; her arthritic hands fumbled at the book of stamps.

Twenty-one days today since poor Walter had died; six stamps gone from the new book of twenty.

Carefully tearing out the seventh she licked it and fixed it to the envelope, and set out on her walk to the mailbox two blocks down the street. On her way she passed by the neighborhood drugstore, with its rows of newspaper racks lined up out front.

When she saw the headlines, Millie began laughing.

TWO

"THE kindness of strangers," Edwina Crusoe mused aloud, "is a remarkably dangerous thing."

She turned to the inside section of the newspaper where the story of last night's events in the hospital continued. Not many facts had been known when the paper went to press, but this lack had been compensated for by the inclusion of some fairly lurid historical sidebars.

The notorious "Fatal Angel" case, for instance, was made much of: in it a nurse had secured the respect of her peers by saving many of her dying patients, in a hospital intensive-care unit where she worked.

She really was a whiz at resuscitation; all her co-workers remarked upon it. And that some patients did not survive was not thought to be her fault; her salvage ratio, after all, was much higher than the hospital's average.

The problem, alas, lay with dying patients themselves: they simply were not numerous enough for her. So she began creating more, and eventually she became ensnared.

A survivor of near-death insisted this nurse had given him some unusual medication, just before he began feeling bad. Other "saved" patients began reporting the same. Soon thereafter the nurse found herself charged with murder and attempted murder, although her attorney still hoped to get her off on manslaughter.

The further chronicled activities of a whole list of deadly doctors, nefarious nurses, and homicidal helpers of every kind dismayed Edwina, not only for the number and variety of nasty things they did but because sick people read newspapers, too. The arrival of a fresh one was a high point in a hospital day, in fact, since call-lights as a rule stayed reliably unlit where newspapers were delivered, until the last want ad, agony column, and obituary notice had been drained of its amusement value.

Which, Edwina thought, meant there must now be patients clamoring at all available exits of Chelsea Memorial Hospital, while those unable to leave would be demanding to draw up their own injections, scrutinizing pills and potions and comparing them suspiciously to ones they remembered—or more worrisomely, did not remember—having been given before.

Sighing, Edwina looked up from the sofa at her own things ranged comfortably in their own places: plump, upholstered club chairs facing one another across the antique chess table, upon it the ivory chess warriors her grandfather Crusoe had brought back from one of his China trips. On the hearth, brass andirons held a trio of cedar logs fragrantly awaiting the touch of the Cape Cod lighter, while from the mantel above gazed a formal portrait of her father, E. R. Crusoe.

Diplomat, industrialist, and paver of the way to wide accord for presidents from Roosevelt to Kennedy and beyond, E. R. in oils was only a little less inclined to small talk than he had been in life. Let the other fellow do the talking, went E. R.'s motto; listening pays better.

Now across from her in E. R.'s red leather armchair, removed from the Litchfield estate to her own apartment after her father's death, Martin McIntyre tossed the sports section aside. "Can I get you something?" he asked hopefully.

Smiling, Edwina settled back into her pillows. He had brought them to her along with an afghan, the paper, and a second glass of sherry; in the kitchen his casserole bubbled merrily and his salad awaited McIntyre's Special Secret Dressing, guaranteed to make even iceberg lettuce taste like garden-fresh leaflings.

"You," she told him, "are coddling me too much. I've spent overnighters in the hospital before, you know. I don't need such intensive care after working just one graveyard shift."

"But I need to give it," he replied, "and you are so self-sufficient, I never get a chance to. Just think of it as good practice for me, in case there ever is a time you can't do for yourself—say, if you should get waterlogged while skin-diving or bruise your hand while changing a tire on that infernal little car of yours."

McIntyre grinned while delivering this advice; not often did he manage to slam dangerous hobbies, fragile sports cars, and her own habitual reluctance to accept help all in the same sentence.

"For a homicide detective, you're a pretty good cook," she remarked half an hour later upon cleaning her plate and offering it for seconds.

"For a ninety-eight-pound woman you're a pretty good eater," he replied, lavishing upon her another helping of cauliflower and cheddar cheese casserole, complete with a nicely browned section of grated-potato crust, a dollop of sour cream, and a biggish slice of garlic bread.

"I saw her today, by the way," he said offhandedly. "The Nash woman, I mean."

Edwina put down her fork. "Really? Why didn't you say so before?" At her feet Maxie the black cat switched his tail, to signal that he was more than willing to try a bit of cauliflower if only it could be accompanied by a bit of cheese.

"Here, Maxie," said McIntyre, dropping his napkin and depositing a spoonful of casserole onto it. "You old culinary adventurer, you."

With a purr of delight Maxie pounced upon his treat.

"I only got a glimpse," McIntyre explained, straightening. "She was going through the gauntlet—pictures, fingerprints, PD intake interview, the whole routine."

"Public defender? You mean they kept her? She's officially charged?"

He shook his head. "District attorney'll decide later what the charges are. Anywhere from battery to manslaughter right on up to the big one—it all depends on how they bargain it."

He took a sip of water, wiped his lips with another napkin and moved back from the table.

"This PD she's got is as useful as a rubber crutch, too. Guy couldn't plead a parking ticket. I wouldn't

26

tell you that, but I knew you'd kill me if you found out I knew and I hadn't."

Edwina stared, indignant. "I don't pester you for details, I never pry about your cases. No matter how juicy they are or how interested I may be, which they are and I am, I never snoop."

"Right," he said, "but this is different. You were there, it's a nurse, and I know you, Edwina. You're worse than Maxie once you get a sniff of something."

Edwina put down her garlic bread, eyeing him. He was tall and hawk-faced with a thin, expressive mouth, courtly manners, and a quick, tenacious intelligence. Incapable of lying, he was not above fibbing at first just to ease her into something.

"Wait a minute, I don't think you only glimpsed this woman."

McIntyre shrugged. "Well, as you just said, I am a homicide detective. And this case is being investigated as a homicide. Possible multiple homicide," he added. "Preliminary statements from relatives of those other two patients are being taken now."

"So it's your case," Edwina said slowly, "and I was a close witness afterwards. Does that mean you have to recuse yourself?"

"Excuse myself," he corrected gently. "Recuse is for judges. And no, I don't think I do."

"But somebody's going to call me to testify, is that it?"

He nodded. "Probably. And any even halfway-decent defense, even the PD team it looks like she's going to have, will think they've found the prize in the Cracker Jacks."

"That I'll have heard things from you that contaminate what I say. Opinions that color my testimony, maybe mess up my memory of what happened. But that's not so bad, Martin. Other people were there, too. Nothing depends on my account of things."

McIntyre nodded again, unhappily. "But there's no guarantee they'll all remember things the same way, and you're the one with the reputation. Face it, Edwina, you're not an unknown anymore. People still remember the Dietz-Claymore case, and in court it'll come out that you've been quietly involved elsewhere, too. Now," he added, "that you've become such a very private duty nurse."

"Practice Limited to Consultation," read her card. It might have read, "Professional Snoop—Medical/Health Matters Only."

People who thought sick relatives were being abused either physically or financially—but couldn't be sure, or couldn't prove it—eventually found their way to Edwina Crusoe. So did invalids whose vulnerabilities ripened them for hucksters and humbugs of every stripe: one such charlatan sold "eternal rest" in the form of nonexistent burial plots, then marketed his mailing list of sick folks to a huge and shameless fraternity of other bamboozlers—or had, until Edwina caught him at it.

"There are lots of possibilities," McIntyre went on. "If your story jibes with what Jillian Nash has to say, prosecution tries to show you're on her side—some sort of sorority-sister slant. If it doesn't, defense implies you're going after the publicity, or that your recollections were tainted by me. They won't need to say you're perjuring yourself, only that you're wrong—and you'll be the one with the high profile."

"I'll be the biggest target, you mean. If my credibility's suspect, it's easier to tear down someone else's. But Martin, who knows at this point if there's even going to be a trial?"

"Oh, I think there is. Jillian Nash insists she doesn't know anything about anything. But the lab found pancuronium in a vial that was supposed to hold Inderal, a heart drug, recovered from her patient's wastebasket. The two other victims will be exhumed for tissue analysis as soon as the court order goes through—by tomorrow or the next day, I expect."

"So the DA thinks he's got three victims," Edwina said.

"Right." He got up, began to clear the table. "Sit," he admonished when she made as if to help him. "It's all on me."

Deftly he carried the plates and glasses to the kitchen, returning a few moments later with coffee, cups, and cream. "So I thought I'd better tell you—" he began.

"To stay right out of this one," Edwina finished for him.

McIntyre looked shocked. "Good heavens, you know me better than that. Not that I see quite how you could be getting further into it. No one's asked you to, I hope, have they?"

Edwina shook her head. "No, thank goodness. It all looks extremely disagreeable, and I'm very glad that none of it's any of my business."

"Good." McIntyre looked relieved; despite his frequent protests to the contrary, he did not really like what he called Edwina's very private nursing duties. A lesser man might even have forbidden them, in the unlikely event any lesser man got the chance to try.

"But," he went on, "however minor your account turns out to be, someone's going to try to tear it down. To reduce it—and you, by the way—to a little pile of bones and hair. So you'd best be prepared, is all I'm saying."

"Oh. Is that all?" Edwina sipped some coffee. "Well, it's a free country. I suppose it's the price we pay."

Privately she did not feel quite so mild about the idea, but having delivered babies, plugged off hemorrhages, propelled food-chunks from the throats of blue-faced choking victims, and given to human beings micrograms of substances so potent they exploded the left ventricles of lab rats to whom, in early FDA tests, they had first been administered, she now found cross-examination a not-unduly-daunting prospect.

"A little pile of bones and hair may have teeth in it," she remarked in summary of her attitude. "And someone else, I think, had best prepare for that."

* * *

Oh, do answer, Edwina thought irritably much later, then realized the ringing telephone was hers and that she lived alone.

It was two A.M. and Martin McIntyre had long since gone home. Bother, she thought, padding barefoot out past the library and the guest room, through the foyer and across the living room to the little cherry desk where the telephone went on shrilling.

"Yes," she demanded, grabbing up the dratted instrument.

At her ankles Maxie twined insistently. "Beat it, you old faker," she told him, "you've been fed twice."

"Hello," shouted someone down the line, "anyone there?"

The call—or preferably the caller—was being strangled somewhere. Finally in a horrid burst of static the voice broke through again.

"Edwina Crusoe?" it shouted. "Awful connection, I'll hang up and call you back."

Oh, good, he would call her back. Not that she got to have any choice about it.

The telephone pealed again. "Edwina Crusoe, who's calling?"

Several electronic clicks were followed by a man's voice so clear it might have been in the next room. Her first thought was that she was extremely glad it wasn't.

"Yes," the voice snapped, "I know who you are. This is Ted B. Nash and I'm busy as hell so let's not waste time. You free?"

Indeed, she thought, only not of you and that can be easily remedied. "Why are you calling me, Mr. Nash?"

"Don't be dense, Miss Crusoe. Jilly says you were there last night." The voice expressed equal parts of impatience, anger, and utter incurable boorishness.

"Jilly," Edwina frowned. Of course. "Jillian Nash."

"Very good," Ted B. Nash snarled. "You are almost as bright as you're advertised. Just put it down," he said to someone in the room with him. "Can't you see I'm having a conversation here?"

No, Edwina thought clearly, you're not.

Hanging up, she set the answering machine to "all" and the volume on the ringer to "silent." Out in the kitchen she bribed Maxie with a chicken leg that had gone past its prime, poured a brandy for herself and stood by the refrigerator drinking it.

I don't need the money, she thought.

Old E. R. had settled an embarrassing number of

millions on her, along with the income of two banks, a textile plant, and an insurance company. Nursing for her was merely a way of being useful, except that for her there was no merely about it. In her fifteen years of nursing it had mattered that she did it, and had mattered that she did it well. And even now that she had retired from hands-on nursing to a less direct sort of caregiving, she felt the same: gobbling up the good things of life without giving any back was a surefire prescription for misery.

And I don't need the aggravation. Ted B. Nash's voice promised plenty of that. He would be the kind who phoned twenty times a day, hectoring and questioning, nitpicking and second-guessing, generally making an almighty nuisance of himself.

Maxie ceased ravaging the chicken leg and began batting it aimlessly around the linoleum, as if to demonstrate that he was no slouch in the nuisance department either, and could he please have some attention? Because if he couldn't, his animal nature might lead him into some even more annoying pastime.

"Oh, all right," she said, swooping down and scooping him. "We'll go back to bed," she told him, "and both sleep very late."

Prutt, said Maxie, gazing adoringly at her.

"And tomorrow morning we'll fix breakfast," she promised, "and eat it watching television, lying around in our pajamas."

Maxie was not in the habit of wearing pajamas; nevertheless he understood the idea of lying around in them very well.

Mrmff, he uttered comfortably, but then his ears pricked up, yellow eye-slits narrowing as he swivelled his velvet head.

Thweep? he asked, leaping down with his tail stiffened into a question mark.

Meeyowrl, he uttered, stalking *en garde* to the apartment door upon which, moments later, someone began hammering: loudly, steadily, and desperately.

"It's late," said the woman at the door, "I know, I'm sorry, but—please, can I come in?"

She was about thirty-five, with thick, short-cropped red hair beginning to get some early strands of silver in it. She wore a pair of faded jeans, sneakers, and a navy sweatshirt-jacket with a hood and a zipper up the front. She didn't look like a woman who cried very often, but she had been doing it recently.

"Please," she said. "My name is Barbara Moran; I'm Jillian Nash's roommate. I'm a nurse, too, I was working a double in the OR up at St. Tom's until two hours ago. We had a long neurosurg case and I didn't find out what happened—"

St. Thomas's Hospital was in Hartford, forty miles away, and an operating room with a head case being done in it was the next best thing to an isolation chamber.

"Miss Moran, I'm not involved in what happened with Jillian. I just happened to be—"

"She didn't do anything," the woman said. "I'm sure of that. But I did, and when the police find out they're going to think she did, too, that she did it *for* me."

"May I see some identification, please?" Edwina said. "I'll need a driver's license, your employee ID from St. Tom's, and something else with your address on it."

The woman handed these over without hesitation.

The picture on the license matched the one on the St. Tom's card; the address matched the address on the checks in the checkbook.

Without apology Edwina flipped to the check register. It was meticulously kept and showed a balance of $875.56. Checks had been written regularly for fuel oil, lights and phone, cable TV, a credit card, a car payment, and another that looked like rent.

"You can't afford me," Edwina said, returning the documents. Unapologetically she named a daily rate for her consultation services; sliding fees, she felt, were for sliding performers.

The woman didn't blink or step back. "One hour," she said. "I can pay you for it now. If after you've heard what I have to say, you still tell me to buzz off, I'll—"

"—go to the police," Edwina finished for her. "You're going to have to do that anyway, you know, if you have information that might help your friend."

Barbara Moran laughed sadly. "No, Miss Crusoe, I won't have to go to the police. The police will come to me—by morning if they're not waiting at my house right now."

So you haven't been home, Edwina thought; you came straight here. Interesting. "How did you know to try me?"

The woman's answering smile made her look all at once quite attractive, like someone whose company would be fun on a hiking trip. Likely she pitched on a softball team or played volleyball in a league, and went out for dinner and a show every Friday night with a half-dozen other professional women. It was the sort of life many nurses led, and one with much to recommend it.

"Sorry," the woman said, "I just can't believe you asked me that. Don't you have any idea how well-known you're getting? I'll bet every nurse in the state has your address and telephone number tucked away somewhere, just in case she ever—"

"Hey," said someone from behind one of the other apartment doors. "Pipe down out there, you women. Middle of the night, you know?"

The effect on Barbara Moran was like a light bulb switching off. "In case anything bad happens," she finished flatly.

So it's not because I was there when Jillian was accused. Combined with McIntyre's comments earlier in the evening, this was a dampening realization. *Fame,* Edwina thought bleakly.

"Are you," said Barbara Moran, "going to let me in or not?"

"You said Jill didn't do anything but you did. What did you mean by that? What exactly did you do?"

Barbara Moran glanced up and down the corridor as if to make sure no eavesdropper had a door cracked open. She frowned down at her sneakers for a moment, then met Edwina's eye squarely.

"I killed my husband," she said.

*   *   *

Ten minutes later Edwina poured fresh coffee into cups.

Out in the living room Barbara Moran sat patiently, showing fatigue only in the way she held her head: perfectly straight, as if she feared any deviation from vertical might make her swoon.

"So you went in for the day shift and stayed for evenings?" Edwina carried the coffee out along with cream and sugar, was not surprised to find Barbara Moran drank it black.

"Yes," the woman said. She sipped coffee. "God, I wish I could mainline that right into an artery. We

35

had two sick calls, and the shift is already short-staffed. And at two o'clock some kid decided to fall out of a tree, landed on his head on a curb."

Edwina grimaced involuntarily. "Subdural?"

"He wishes. Cord transsection plus a big intra-cranial bleed. By the time they got his neck sta-bilized so they could get him in the CAT-scanner, his whole left brain was moved over."

Barbara Moran shook her head. "Hope he wasn't planning on being an athlete. Or," she added, "a rocket scientist. But he's alive and of course his parents are overjoyed. For now. Later it's going to be another story, of course, when they figure out how little is really left of him."

She looked up guiltily, seeming to realize how this sounded. "Sorry. Battle fatigue. I transferred to OR when I couldn't be nice to patients anymore. Just ran out of niceness, you know? The well ran dry. But now I only have to see them when they're un-conscious, and it all works out very well."

Edwina nodded; it wasn't the first time she had heard that story. Burnout blues: the variations were endless. But they were all beside the point at this moment, and besides, at three A.M. Edwina was not in the mood for a game of Ain't It Awful.

"You said you killed your husband. You weren't convicted of any crime, though?" Conviction of a felony was flat grounds for losing a nursing license, and without a valid license a nurse couldn't work.

"That's right," Barbara Moran said. "I shot him with a twenty-two target pistol. But he was swinging a tire iron at the time. At me. Fractured my skull, my shoulder, and three of my ribs. And so much," she finished wryly, "for court orders of protection."

"I see. And what's that got to do with what's going on now with Jillian?"

36

Barbara Moran shrugged. "It was nearly ten years ago, but people in my home town still think I'm a murderer." The town she named was familiar: lots of high-school football championships, not much work for the dads of the football players now that the brass mills and tire plants had all shut down.

"He was the fair-haired boy," Barbara Moran said. "Great at sports, real good-looking, related to half the population. They said I must have done something to make him so mad. I did, too," she finished softly. "I existed."

She picked up her cooling coffee, swallowed some. "And I wasn't completely honest with you about Jillian, just now. She's not just my roommate. We've lived together three years. I hope that doesn't shock you."

It didn't, but it explained more of why Moran was worried. "You are in trouble," Edwina said. "The papers will love this."

Moran nodded. "Anyway, we haven't been getting along, Jill and I. It's been coming for a while, but three weeks ago I told her I was thinking of finding another place. Since then she's been doing things to try to change my mind."

"What sort of things?"

Moran looked uncomfortable. "Silly things at first. Funny greeting cards, ambitious dinners. Or they would be silly if they weren't so sad."

"Because they weren't working."

"No. So she upped the ante, started talking about buying a house. Her father would lend her the money, we could have a pool and a tennis court. I wouldn't have to work, she said. I could take care of the place and she'd bring home the paycheck."

Edwina tipped her head. "An attractive proposition. Always assuming she could back it up—and that you were for sale."

"Exactly. And I wasn't. Then about ten days ago she wrote me one of those desperate begging letters that make you feel like you just crawled out from under a rock. In it she said she'd do anything—lie, steal, even kill—if only I wouldn't leave."

"I see. Do you still have it?"

Barbara Moran shook her head. "No. I gave it back to her. I told her she should never trust anyone that much, to put things like that on paper. I think she still has it, though."

And so it would likely be found among her possessions.

"Also," Barbara Moran said, digging in the canvas tote she carried, "she's been getting *these*. One a day all this week. She tried to hide them, but I found them in the trash. I've been carrying them around, trying to figure out what to do about them."

She held out six envelopes. Each contained a sheet of yellow notebook paper bearing a dozen lines of block-printing in blue ballpoint pen.

All the messages expressed, crudely and forcefully, a single emotion: hatred. They flatly accused Jillian Nash of getting away with murdering someone named Walter Clemens. None of them bore a return address or signature.

"Someone sounds pretty convinced. Who's this Walter person Jill's supposed to have killed?"

Barbara Moran sighed. "He was a patient of Jillian's who died on her shift, three weeks ago. His wife wouldn't believe it was plain cardiac arrest. She raised all sorts of a fuss. Said she saw Jillian reset his IV rate, and I guess she still hasn't gotten rid of the idea that that's what killed him, somehow."

"But Jill wasn't suspected of really doing anything wrong. Not officially, I mean."

"Not then. You can see how it's going to look now, though. Like maybe she tried something out on him, and got away with it."

Edwina nodded slowly. It was going to look, in fact, a good deal worse than that. "Barbara, is there something else you're not being honest about? You didn't encourage Jillian at all, for instance, in her fantasy of doing something that would bind you to her somehow?"

The little gold clock on the cherry desk chimed once: three forty-five. Curled on the seat of the red leather chair Maxie sighed, paws twitching, and slept again.

Barbara Moran shook her head. "I swear I didn't. I thought she was just desperate, saying things she didn't mean. It's why I gave the letter back, because I felt sorry for her."

"And now?"

"You mean now what do I think, or now how do I feel?"

"Both. Your hour's almost up, by the way." And you haven't yet, Edwina added silently, told me what you want.

"Now," said Moran, "I'm in a nightmare. I know Jill. She's a little tightly wound, I'll grant that much. But she could no more really hurt anyone than— well. Only it's going to look so much as if she has, you see. And I'll be in the news again," she finished miserably, "on account of it."

"Guilt by association?"

"Of course, and both ways—me because I'm associated with her, and her because of my past. If only you could show that she didn't do anything, we might be able to go on living our lives. But if not . . ."

"I understand," Edwina said. "Otherwise you'll have to live it down all over again."

Moran took a last sip of coffee. "Right. And there's one other thing. If Jill didn't do it, which I'm certain she didn't, then someone else did. Someone who's still out there taking care of sick people. Giving them," she finished, "their medicine."

Barbara Moran got up. "I may not be the best nurse in the world myself, Miss Crusoe, but that thought makes my skin crawl."

"Laying it off on Jill," Edwina said thoughtfully. "It is an interesting scenario, I must admit. I don't quite see how the thing could be accomplished, though. The logistics of it would be so difficult. Or what the purpose would be."

The little clock struck four. "How much do I owe you?" Moran asked resignedly, fishing the checkbook once more from her tote bag.

"What?" Edwina blinked. "Oh. Nothing. I told you before, you can't afford me. And neither can Jillian; not on her salary, anyway. Not unless she touched her father for that loan."

Moran made a sound of exasperation. "She won't, not now. For a house she would; there's collateral in that so she'd know she could pay it back if he got snotty about it. The man's impossible. But not just to spend, especially not on something like this. He'd hold it over her forever."

Which, Edwina thought, he was probably still going to get a chance to do, unless Ted Nash meant to let his daughter languish in the care of a public defender who couldn't plead a parking ticket.

"You know," she said, "I'm not a lawyer. People pay me to find things out and usually I do. But I decide what else happens to the information after my clients get it, and sometimes they end up not liking that part

40

of the arrangement. I mean," she explained, "you can buy my research abilities but my silence is not included in the deal, if what I find out is bad. And the police know that, too, that I won't conceal evidence."

"What do I care?" Barbara Moran asked bitterly as she headed for the door. "I can't afford you either way. Or so *you* say."

Edwina gazed across the room, at the small cherry desk where the answering machine's light now blinked energetically. Looking at it, she came to her decision.

Aggravating, but interesting. And if by chance someone else really had done the deeds . . . well, maybe the thing could use a bit of poking into.

"Right," she confirmed a final time, "you can't." As if triggered by her gaze, the answering machine clicked faintly and its tiny tape began turning, recording yet another attempt at an incoming call.

"But Ted B. Nash can," she added, "and I'll bet that's him now."

* * *

There, Millie Clemens thought, sealing the third envelope. Ignoring Hiram Greenspan's knock-out drops, she had sat up half the night working on the messages, deciding exactly what and how much she should say.

Too little and the letters would be ignored. Millie knew well how grief elbowed all else aside, until even words spoken straight into one's face had barely a chance of being understood.

Too much, though, and she gave away the show. Having been rejected already by the hospital and the police, she had learned her lesson: no one would help her unless she had something big to offer them in return, something they couldn't get otherwise.

Walter would have helped her, of course, but Walter was dead. Of—her lips twisted bitterly—natural causes. After the autopsy the hospital's lawyer made this clear, speaking slowly and using simple words as if she were some idiot child while she sat there and fought to keep herself from slapping him.

The lawyer had had an egg-spot on his tie. A bit of bacon had been stuck between his teeth. Remembering this, Millie remembered too the faint cedary smell of Walt's good blue suit, when she'd slipped it from its hanger for the undertaker to put on him.

So: no promises, nothing told. But enough hints to get her in on discussions those other loved ones might be preparing to have, the other survivors now mourning their own losses. Talks about lawsuits and damages and making the hospital pay.

And about punishing the nurse. Millie hadn't the resources to hire a lawyer on her own; she had consulted several of them, but the lack of evidence was such that none would take her case on contingency, all she could afford.

Now, though, there were going to be scads of lawyers, along with lots of other people suffering just as she was. More than anything Millie wanted to be with them, to hear them say aloud what she continued saying silently: that some murdering nurse had killed her dearest one, probably just for the fun of it. After all, what other reason could there be?

Gazing at her little pile of letters, Millie Clemens felt sure that the people who read them would understand. Grieving and furious just as she was, they would not look down on her or take her for a fool.

They would want to hear what she had to say, and to hear it they would take her in with them.

More than anything, Millie looked forward to that.

42

THREE

"THE moment of death," said Anne Crain, "is an appealing fiction with no resemblance to the facts."

Six hours had passed since Edwina's interview with Barbara Moran. In that time she had spoken at length with Ted B. Nash, who began by issuing a string of orders like the bully-boss of some rowdy chain gang.

Patient probing by Edwina, however, had uncovered in Nash a gift for the salient point, which was that his only daughter was in deep and serious trouble, while Edwina was proposing, if not necessarily to get her out of it, then at least to learn whether and how this task might be accomplished.

"All right," Nash had finished grudgingly, "I'll wire you a check. But I want regular progress reports, I want daily—"

"Mr. Nash," she had interrupted him, "how would you rather I spend my expensive time? In doing the necessary, or in toadying up to you?"

There was a brief transoceanic silence on the telephone, then a surprised and rueful laugh. In that moment Edwina liked Ted Nash very much.

"Let me know if you need anything," he'd said in another tone entirely. "And let me know the lay of the land, too, will you? If you can, when you find out. If she's all right, I mean. If she's . . ."

"Won't you," Edwina queried carefully, "be asking her?"

But Ted B. Nash needed no kid-glove handling on that score. "Miss Crusoe, my daughter and I haven't been on terms since her mother died eight years ago. Jillian didn't call me about this problem. She called my lawyer, who alerted me, and I trust that answers your question?"

It did. By the end of the conversation, in fact, Edwina thought she and Nash understood each other very well. He wanted information and she had been engaged to supply it, which suited her precisely. That she had no axe to grind in the matter only made that information more likely—to her mind, as well as to his—to be reliable. She had hung up feeling well-pleased.

Now Anne Crain peered at her from a desk in the small grey office of the pathology department, in the basement of Chelsea Memorial Hospital. Spread before her were a half-dozen hospital charts of the patients upon whom she was due to perform postmortem exams.

Ex-patients, someone else might have said, but Anne would not have said it even as a joke. Behind her on open shelves were heaps of professional journals, stacks of bound monographs, and neat piles of articles Xeroxed from the medical library.

"Imagine a standing row of dominoes a billion pieces long," Anne Crain mused. "Now start at either end and push one over, or go to the middle and push two in opposite directions."

Beside her desk stood a typing table; on it squatted the old Underwood typewriter that Anne refused to give up. The piece she was writing was entitled "To Do No Harm: Autopsy and the Physician's Oath."

"They all fall down," Anne Crain said, "but at which moment is the row destroyed—when you push the first domino, or when the final one falls? Isn't it a row of dominoes even then? What has it really lost, I wonder, but its ability to fall?"

She stopped short. "Never mind, Edwina, I shouldn't force my obsessions on you when you're nice enough to visit. They're starting to call me 'Crazy Annie' around here; did you know that?"

Edwina did know, and thought it most unfair. Had Anne been a cardiologist her obsession with her specialty would have gone unremarked or at worst thought eccentric. But a forty-year-old woman with a passion for the dead was just too exotic for her colleagues, other MDs most of whom were by nature as unmoving in their opinions as Anne's patients were on their mortuary slabs.

"I don't see why I shouldn't be interested in what I do," she complained, "although considering the general intellectual level in this place. . . ."

She laughed sadly. "In general, though, they leave me pretty much alone, so I guess I shouldn't gripe."

But being left alone, Edwina thought, was the heart of Anne Crain's trouble. The ability to disassemble a human body and to reassemble it again was not exactly tops on most people's list of social skills, and talking about it wasn't on the list at all.

Nevertheless it was the only skill Anne had as well as her only interest, so getting her to discuss it was like dropping a quarter in a jukebox: easy to start but hard to stop. As a result most people avoided her altogether.

Now she'd gone off into a detailed, picturesque description of an occult myxomatous tumor she'd discovered while hunting for mitral-valve vegetation in the heart of a deceased heroin addict.

"Like a pearl in an oyster," she enthused, "just sitting in there waiting for me to come along and—"

"What," Edwina interrupted gently, "pushed the domino?"

Anne Crain blinked. "What? Oh, of course. That's why you called in the first place, wasn't it? Come on in, I'll show you. This one's turning out to be extremely interesting, actually."

She got up from behind her desk. In her green scrub dress, white lab coat, and white utility shoes, she resembled a model for a medical-uniforms catalogue: slim, blonde, and wholesome.

"The medical resident saved some lovely blood samples drawn during the resuscitation attempt," she said. "Puts us way ahead of schedule on the toxicology reports."

As she spoke she led Edwina through a pair of sulfur-yellow doors into a large, chilly room resembling an operating room—except of course that it contained no anesthesia equipment, the ultimate painkiller for patients transported here having already been delivered.

At one end of the room was a bank of a dozen tall metal refrigerator doors, to one side of them a row of four brushed-aluminum sinks whose faucets and soap-dispensers were controlled by foot-pedals. On shelves above the sinks sat boxes of surgical masks and paper caps, paper shoe covers and rubber gloves in various sizes. Pairs of clear plastic safety glasses hung by black elastic straps from hooks on the wall, while surgical gowns and plastic aprons were dispensed from a deep-drawered cart.

The reek of preservative in the room was astonishing, strong as chloroform but not as sweet. With the stink came memories of the fetal pig Edwina had dissected in nursing school: pink flesh yellowed and stiffened, slipperily fixed in a chemical limbo of non-decay and sealed obscenely in a plastic bag.

"Ghastly, isn't it?" Anne Crain said cheerfully. "I always say I'd rather have normal rot than that."

At the room's center stood four procedure tables, each equipped with a headrest, overhead lamps, and a sink into which grooves on the table sloped gently. Three of the tables were vacant; on the fourth lay the sheet-draped body of Berenice Bennington.

"Modern embalming, what a beastly idea," Anne Crain went on as she drew back the modesty-preserving cloth. "Pickling whole people in chemicals, gad, it's barbaric. Who'd want to last that long?"

"You don't embalm them here, do you?" Edwina glanced about; from the thickness of the preserving-fluid stench it seemed the walls and floor must recently have been sluiced down in the stuff.

"No," Anne said, "just tissue specimens. But the medical school's cadavers are right next door until the students finish with them. They keep them in tanks, and the atmosphere, I'm afraid, is rather penetrating."

"Oh," said Edwina faintly, averting her mind's eye from this information, which was more than she had really wanted to know.

"Sorry, Berenice," Anne added to the body on the

table, "but it's just us girls and I want to show something to Edwina."

The body of Berenice Bennington, who appeared to have been perhaps seventy years old, was greyish white. Purplish-red livor mortis stained the flanks and buttocks and the backs of the arms and thighs. These stains came from pooling of the body's blood after death, and were entirely normal. The big blue bruise on the breastbone was not normal, however, nor were the puncture marks that peppered it liberally; neither had the purplish hole in the left external jugular come from any natural cause.

These, rather, were the stigmata of resuscitation, never a genteel procedure and in this case apparently less so than usual: fractured ribs where the heel of a hand had tried compressing the heart between the sternum and thoracic spine, punctures where drugs had been shot straight into the stalled cardiac muscle.

Someone had tried to get a big IV line into that jugular, stabbing it with a trochar the size of a knitting needle; by the telltale single hole, the first attempt had been successful, or too late to make a second try worthwhile.

"I wouldn't mind being stuffed with spices, though, like the Egyptians used to do," Anne Crain went on conversationally as she moved to the other side of the examination table.

The body's face had a slightly mashed-looking appearance, the nose a bit flattened and cheeks pushed out-of-round where an oxygen mask had been pressed to them.

"Imagine," Anne said, "going through eternity smelling of cinnamon and cloves, lavender and eucalyptus. Like being buried in your grandmother's

48

linen closet. Anyway, here's the old scar from her graft surgery."

She pointed midline on the body's chest. "I ran my incision alongside so as not to obliterate it. Her coronary vessels were patent, grafts nice and clean, one old infarct in the ventricle."

She reached down and grasped the body's left arm, turning and extending it. "So she didn't have a myocardial infarction, and the microscope confirms that. When the drug screens came in I wondered. She did have evidence of an old stroke, and her chart notes complete anosmia as well as the loss of her sense of taste. The stroke," Anne explained, "was in the part of her brain that processes taste and smell, and as a result of it those senses were knocked out permanently, according to her records. But look, Edwina, this is the other thing I wanted you to see."

Frowning, Edwina stepped forward. Why would Anne suspect a heart attack on a murder victim, or at least on an apparent one?

Perhaps the most startling thing about the body was how normal it looked, considering that almost all of its internal organs had been removed for sectioning and microscopic scrutiny. The tiny silk sutures Anne had used for closing the autopsy incision, beginning at the suprasternal notch and dividing to a Y shape on the abdomen, did not at all resemble the gross black mattress stitches favored both for sturdiness and speed by most pathologists, as after all the patient would hardly complain of any scar.

Delicately Anne lifted Berenice Bennington's arm. "This was her IV site before the emergency began. See anything?"

The flesh inside the elbow was puffed and red-dened; above and below the IV needle's puncture mark, a small incision had been made, then repaired with stitches fine and pale as hairs.

"Her IV infiltrated," Edwina said, recognizing the site of a postmortem tissue biopsy. "I don't quite see . . ."

"What difference that makes," Anne Crain finished for her. "Of course not. Very few people die from needles coming out of veins and dripping a little IV fluid into the surrounding tissue. The worst they get is a hot, sore arm for a while. But what if, for instance, there's potassium in an infiltrated IV line?"

"Then they get a fat or muscle necrosis," Edwina answered promptly, "from the drug leaking into the tissue and sitting there, eating away."

"Precisely." Lowering the arm to the table, Anne nodded her professorial approval.

"Sitting there in tissue and in plasma," she said, "which is why I made that little incision—to find it, if it was there. Which I did."

She pursed her lips thoughtfully, gazing at the body on the table. "The IV must have infiltrated early in the resuscitation," she said slowly, "or there would have been more edema. Someone saw the line wasn't running, removed it, and started a new one in her right hand. The new line was still present when the body got here, and it confused me until I found inflammation in the left arm and realized what it was."

"The old IV site," said Edwina, "the one she had before the emergency began."

Anne Crain agreed. "Into which an offending sub-stance was injected—a paralytic drug whose presence is particularly hard to confirm by lab analysis, or was until a few months ago."

She paused to look into the body's slack and bloodless face. "And that, my friend, is what I found in your arm: pancuronium, a drug you never should have gotten, and which I ought not to have found in the fatty tissues around your intravenous site."

She pulled the sheet back up. "The drug pancuronium breaks down in minutes to succinic acid and choline. They're normal substances in the body, so finding them doesn't always mean you have also found evidence of pancuronium administration."

She began moving toward her office door. "The amount of the drug that doesn't get broken down almost at once is very small, so pancuronium used to be one of those drugs that's almost impossible to detect. But some bright people out in California found a way to use a gas chromatograph and mass spectrometry, so now you can pick out two nanograms of the stuff in a milliliter of plasma, even in spun-down serum from a pulverized tissue prep. That's what I used, the tissue her IV needle leaked the dosed fluid into."

"So we know she got the drug, and we know she got it through that intravenous," Edwina said as she followed Anne Crain back into her little office.

"Right," Anne replied. "That much is rather clear. What's not clear is why it killed her, or even that it did."

To Edwina's stare she returned an impatient I-can't-help-it grimace. "Well, think about it, Edwina, the woman gets the dose and she stops breathing. That's normal, that's what the drug's supposed to

51

do, and of course the absence of breathing will kill anybody if it lasts long enough, right?"

Anne's eyes narrowed. "Except it didn't last long enough. How could it have? The woman's in a hospital, the drug's not poison in itself, the alarm was raised almost instantly as far as I can see from the resuscitation note, and an on-call anesthesia resident's got her breathing again inside of three minutes."

"Less," Edwina said. "She was being ventilated with a mask from the code cart before anesthesia got there. It was a pretty well-run event, as those things go."

Anne Crain shrugged impatiently. "Well, then it's all the more odd. People get this stuff all the time in the OR, and in the intensive care units while they're on ventilators. They don't die of it, so how come Berenice did?"

Edwina thought for a moment. "I don't know," she admitted. "What do you think happened?"

Anne made a face. "When I tell you, you'll be calling me crazy too. But frankly, I think the pancuronium is some sort of red herring, and I'm pretty sure she died of something else. That's how I'll fill out the autopsy report, too—'cause of death unknown pending investigation.'"

"You mean another drug?" Which would be extremely curious, because if Berenice Bennington hadn't died of a dose of pancuronium then Jill Nash could hardly have killed her with it, could she? But in that case what was the point of Berenice's getting it, or of Jill having the empty vial in her pocket?

"I don't know," Anne said. "I've put that woman's remains through every toxicological screen you've ever heard of, and more that you haven't. Nothing there, but I'm still not satisfied."

"Uh-oh." *Someone else*, Barbara Moran had said, *still out there taking care of patients. Giving them their medicine.*

"Anne, is there any such thing nowadays as a completely undetectable poison?"

Anne Crain shrugged. "Books'll tell you no," she said, "but if you ask me, it looks as if there is one now."

* * *

"I don't," said Jill Nash, "want you here. You can tell my father to keep his so-called help. He only wants to gloat and say all my problems are Barbara's fault—oh, why don't you all just go away? I didn't do anything, why can't anybody believe me?"

It was just past noon, and in the living room of the little house where Jill Nash lived with Barbara Moran a color TV set was broadcasting a soap opera. The rest of the furnishings were Sears early-American: dark pine, matching plaid upholstery, braided rug. In a tapestry bag by the recliner facing the big TV, a needlepoint project was neatly stowed; the design on the canvas was of an eagle with an olive branch in its beak.

"Jill, please just talk to her," Barbara Moran pleaded. "I can't stand seeing you this way."

"You," said Jill Nash stonily, "can't stand seeing me at all." She turned her face back to the television.

Barbara sighed. She was wearing a navy sweatshirt, jogging pants, and running shoes. A terry sweatband held back her thick red hair.

"I have to go," she said in tones of strained patience, "I'm due at work. She's been like this since she came home," she added helplessly.

Nodding, Edwina stepped past her into the room. Wrapped in a quilt, Jill lay on the sofa in a clutter of

53

magazines and used tissues; on the table beside her were several empty soda cans, an Entenmann's coffee-cake box with part of a cake still in it—Jill's idea of comfort food, apparently—and a bottle of liquid cold medicine.

Edwina considered reminding her that without her father's help—and the quarter-million-dollar bond he'd raised on quite short notice—she would still be sitting in jail. The public defender, too, had been sent packing in favor of a top-gun criminal lawyer whose practice leaned toward high-visibility crimes, the kind committed either by or against wealthy famous people. Unfortunately, according to Barbara, Jill despised him on sight, although at the moment she apparently despised almost everyone.

"I know who you are," she said without taking her eyes off the television screen, "you're some sort of rich-girl busybody who goes around sticking her nose where it doesn't belong. Why don't you go throw a fancy party or something, stay out of my business?"

She sniffled, then yawned. By the amount of cold medicine gone out of the bottle Edwina thought Jill was lucky to be alive, much less awake; the stuff was formulated according to the no brain/no pain theory of therapeutic pharmacology, easing discomfort by the simple method of obliterating consciousness.

Jill glanced sideways, saw her looking. "Oh, and I suppose we disapprove of that too, don't we? Naughty, naughty, abusing our medicines." She snatched up the bottle, took a defiant swig.

"Want some?" she invited. Without makeup, her unwashed hair hanging in lank strands, Jill looked younger and less innocent than she had two nights before. In her pale, pinched face, her eyes were like those of some trapped animal, bright with fear and misery.

"No, thank you," Edwina said quietly, "but I'd love a cup of coffee, if that's not too much trouble."

Jill frowned. In order to supply the refreshment she would have to get up, and she was not quite rude enough to refuse. "All right," she grumbled, "I'll make coffee. But then you have to go. I'm sick, I feel terrible, I feel like I'm going to die."

Considering the amount of diphenhydramine she'd swallowed, Edwina thought that was no wonder. Clad in pajamas and slippers Jill padded toward the kitchen; as she did so Edwina dropped the cold-medicine bottle into her purse.

The kitchen was a clean, bright haven with geraniums blooming in the windows, copper pans glinting from the walls. An ancient, round-shouldered Frigidaire thrummed to itself in one corner; in the other an old gas stove hunkered comfortably, a red teakettle perched in readiness upon one burner.

"Look, Jill," she said as the coffee maker began burbling on the counter, "I realize you're in a lot of pain, here, but—"

"Oh, you do, do you?" Jill snapped. "Well, that's a big fat comfort. I'll sure sleep a lot better knowing you sympathize."

She got out mugs and milk, swayed woozily, and straightened with an effort. "Yes, sir, that makes me feel a whole bunch better. Too bad it doesn't do me any good."

Without warning her grin fell apart. Standing in the middle of the linoleum, clutching a mug in one hand and a carton of milk in the other, Jill Nash began to weep in great wrenching sobs.

"But I didn't *do* it, I *didn't*, and they put me in that

awful place with those *awful* women, prostitutes and thieves, and I didn't know if—"

Edwina took the mug and carton and steered her to a chair, whereupon Jill laid her head on the kitchen table and cried hard.

Jill, Edwina realized as she found the downstairs bathroom and wrung a clean washcloth in cold water, had never been in trouble before—not bad trouble, anyway. Not the kind where they put you in an awful place with a lot of awful women and possibly even left you there, which was the fate the girl was now imagining.

It hadn't occurred to her yet that it could be worse. The key phrase was depraved indifference, for which if there were no mitigating circumstances the penalty in Connecticut could be death.

Edwina could not think of any circumstance that mitigated killing hospital patients, especially by a nurse in charge of caring for them. She doubted whether being a lesbian could be seen as one, no matter how many psychologists Ted B. Nash paid to stand up and say it was so; there were too many nonmurdering lesbians in the world for a court to swallow that idea readily.

All of which still lay quite far in the future, and none of which was part of Edwina's business. Mine is just to reason why, she reminded herself, glimpsing her own lean, thoughtful face in the bathroom mirror. All I want are the facts.

But at this her large, dark eyes looked skeptical, for the facts so invariably arrived—as they were arriving now—with actual living people attached to them: people who at least on their surfaces were much like oneself, and with whose pains one could hardly help identifying.

After all, she admonished herself, if we had to de-

56

serve kind treatment, we might none of us get much. Still, as she gave the washcloth a final glum twist, she could not help wondering if she was comforting a murderess, for there was certainly something very odd about Jill Nash, something repellent although not quite identifiable that set Edwina's teeth unhappily on edge.

"Now," she said, handing the cloth to Jill and watching her press it to her face, "I want you to listen to me. I don't work for you or for Barbara. You can't fire me and neither can she, understand? You don't have any say in what I do."

Jill nodded. Her tears had ended; now she straightened in her chair. "But my father—"

"Your father isn't paying me to snoop into your life." It crossed her mind that this, to Jill, must be the sticking point: her father's objections to the way she lived, and her resistance to his bullying or snooping on the topic.

"Nor," she went on, "do I plan reporting on your romantic situation. If he wants to know, let him find out himself."

The ghost of a cautious smile touched Jill's bitten lips. "I've been saying that for years."

"But what I do mean to find out," Edwina went on, "is what happened the other night. Whether," she added as Jill's look hardened, "you like it or not, and whether it's to your advantage or not. Do you see? Do you understand what I'm doing, now?"

Jill frowned. "You mean if you thought I killed that woman and the others, you'd say so? To my father, or the police?"

Edwina shook her head. "No. I don't report my thoughts. But if I learned some fact I thought the police should know, I'd tell them. I'd just tell your father first—it's the only way I work, and it's the arrangement he's agreed to."

"I don't get it," Jill protested. "What's the point of—wait a minute, I see, you could get in trouble yourself, couldn't you? If you hid things. But why would my father pay you to—"

She stopped, eyes widening in realization. "He must think I didn't do it, and that's what you'll find out. Otherwise—but he hasn't seen me in over five years. How could he be so sure?"

"Maybe he remembers you," Edwina suggested quietly. "Maybe he knows something about you that I don't."

Or maybe not, she thought, wondering why she kept treating this woman like a child. Was it only that Jill looked so much like one now, pale and frightened and big-eyed? Or was she responding to some subtle lack, something missing in Jill's whole affect that she still could not quite put her finger on?

Certainly, Jill was reading her father's motives with utter incorrectness. Ted Nash's actions owed much more to an instinct for damage control, Edwina felt sure, than to any confidence in his daughter's innocence.

"Anyway," she said, "I came here to ask you just one thing. How long was it between the time you left Mrs. Bennington's room and the time her niece came out after you? I know," she added, "other people have asked you. But I want to hear it from you."

Jill winced, remembering. "Uh-huh. They asked me. And I know, because I'd just given the man in 706 a dose of Demerol."

"What," Edwina asked, "has that got to do with it?"

The girl—not a girl, Edwina reminded herself—shrugged. "Well, he'd had a toe amputated and he was in a lot of pain. So I gave him the Demerol, but as I was going into Mrs. Bennington's room I heard him still moaning."

She frowned. "I hate it when they moan. Anyway, I looked at my watch and only five minutes had gone by, so I thought it might take longer for the Demerol to work, but if it didn't I'd give him a little morphine. He had that ordered, too."

"I see," Edwina said. "Then what?"

"Then I came out of Mrs. Bennington's room and I heard him again, and now it had been fifteen minutes, which if Demerol was going to work it should have by then. So I went to the desk, got the medication room keys out of the drawer, drew up the morphine, put the keys back in the drawer, and brought it back. And when I did that I looked at my watch again so I could put the time down on the controlled-substances sheet."

So far, this made perfect sense. Morphine was often ordered in case Demerol turned out not to be enough. And although the med-room keys did not belong in a drawer at the nursing desk—they belonged on a chain around the neck or in the pocket of the charge nurse, and nowhere else—the drawer was where the keys were very often found, as chasing after the charge nurse every time you wanted them was a nuisance, especially on the short-staffed night shift.

"Anyway," said Jill, "it was just five minutes from when I heard him the second time to when I wrote the morphine dose on the sheet. And as I was writing, Mrs. Bennington's niece started screaming, and the rest I guess you know."

Edwina guessed she did. She also knew how long it took for a dose of pancuronium to run through an IV volutrol, flow through the tubing into the patient's circulation, and be deposited in tissues in quantities sufficient to cause noticeable paralysis:

About five minutes. Which pretty much ruled out the thought that had sprung to Edwina's mind when Anne Crain asked the question: why had Berenice Bennington died in spite of such quick resuscitation efforts?

The thought had taken the form of a most uncharitable mental picture of Mrs. Bennington's niece, sitting there waiting for the drug to take effect after having somehow given it herself. It was a picture that answered Anne Crain's question rather nicely, except that now the timing had turned out to be impossible. Miss Bennington had come out too soon.

The idea carried with it several other knotty difficulties, the most minor of which being how Mrs. Bennington's niece could have gotten hold of the drug in the first place. Pancuronium was not a controlled substance, as it was clearly not suitable for abuse. Neither, however, was it left lying around.

No, the idea would not serve. For one thing it could not have been accomplished in the time available; for another, the drug was not easy to acquire. Finally, the theory failed to explain how or why two earlier victims had died, when Mrs. Bennington's niece had not been present in the hospital at all.

And when Jill Nash *had* been: taking care of them, giving them their medicines. As she thought this, a realization struck Edwina: the quality Jill was missing. Like feeling for a pulled tooth, she thought; such a small gap, yet so shockingly, almost disorientingly vacant.

"How," she asked, "do you feel now? I don't mean about you being in trouble. I mean about them, the three who've died."

Upstairs the shower hissed off; footsteps moved across the floor as Barbara Moran readied herself for another nursing shift at St. Tom's.

Jill Nash looked up, her gaze flat and incurious. "What do you mean, feel about them? I've been trying to tell you I didn't have anything to do with it. Why should I feel anything?"

The name of the quality was compassion.

*　　*　　*

In cases of suspected homicide when the putative victim had already been buried, the first material step toward accomplishing exhumation in the state of Connecticut was taken by a clerk in the investigative office of the attorney general.

The clerk, at the direction of a deputy attorney, sent a request to superior court stating why the peace that ordinarily passeth all understanding ought in this case to be interrupted by a backhoe.

Once a court order for disinterment had been issued, copies were distributed: to the next of kin, if any; to the licensed funeral director responsible for transporting the body; to the pathologist, usually a state medical examiner, who would examine it; to the officers investigating the suspected homicide; and to the sexton of the cemetery in the town where a grave was to be opened.

Thus it was that five days after James C. Milton was buried in the northwest corner of Hillside Cemetery, before the salmon-colored gladioli and the yellow and white chrysanthemums that blanketed his resting place had even finished wilting, the sexton of the cemetery in the little town of North Branford put on his woolen hat, took a final gulp of his morning coffee, and went irritably out to supervise the chore of digging James C. Milton right back up again.

Thus it was also that Edwina drove to the cemetery on that October morning, one day after visiting Anne Crain and Jill Nash, and saw the sexton stalking toward her across a still-green lawn, which under his flinty stewardship would never dare sprout a weed.

The cemetery was a neatly kept acre with a low fieldstone wall all around it and an enormous maple tree precisely at its center. Directly beneath the tree, the oldest stone in the yard was a marble slab inscribed with the name Zebediah Scott and the dates 1764–1805. The air smelled of wet leaves, wood smoke, and bitter, ancient tears.

"Lot of damned unnecessary foolishness this is," the sexton groused upon spying Edwina a little apart from the group gathered near the most recent grave. "Fellow's dead, ain't he?"

The sexton, Walter Bengston, was the sort of dour Yankee who when St. Peter called his name would reply "Ayuh." He had been head gardener on the Crusoe place for years before retiring here to North Branford, where he kept himself busy cultivating hybrid rhododendrons, supervising the graveyard, and subjecting town activities to his constant, constitutionally skeptical scrutiny.

"All right, Jerry," he called now. "Might as well get it done with."

At this a younger fellow in jeans, work boots, and a plaid shirt climbed into a miniature backhoe that stood idling nearby. Thick, black fumes belched in a smelly cloud from the machine as it clattered forward, its engine giving out a deep, bone-rattling rumble.

"Be lucky if we don't wake 'im 'fore we raise 'im," Walter Bengston observed sourly through the din.

He shook his head, upon which he wore a bright red wool cap of the type ordinarily favored by deer hunters. As it was not yet December, the earflaps of the cap were not yet pulled down.

"Town engineer's all het up for it, though," he went on in a down-East-flavored twang. If you stuck a hole in Walter, Edwina thought, he would bleed maple syrup.

"Got a triple-action boom, twelve-inch rubber track, and a four-cylinder, liquid-cooled overhead diesel engine, hydrostatic drive train, not to mention a deluxe, high-back reclining seat," he said. His tone communicated just what he thought of all these newfangled amenities, and of the whippersnapper engineer who had frittered away perfectly good town tax money on them, too.

Inside the machine's cab Jerry worked levers energetically, grinning like a kid with a new toy truck. Jerkily the backhoe's scoop-shaped blade reached down, then bit with a shriek of stones on metal into the loose earth mounded atop James Milton's grave.

"Widow's all upset," Walter Bengston observed unhappily as the first shovelful of earth rained onto the graveyard lawn.

"My wife, some other women from the grange are sitting home with her," he added. "You here with those folks?"

He angled his head at the five men waiting by the hearse's open tailgate, in the little gravel drive that faded to hardpan as it wound through the cemetery: the funeral director, his assistant, a reporter from the *Register*, Martin McIntyre, and another plain-clothes officer whom Edwina did not know.

It occurred to her that Walter had just spoken more words in fifteen minutes than she had ever heard him speak before in her life. Perhaps he was nervous over this project of digging up a dead man, even on a morning so bright that the air seemed positively carbonated with sunshine.

Another load of grave dirt fell from the backhoe's bladed mouth. The hole looked to be about four feet deep now, and the earth in the pile rising beside it was darker, heavier, and more claylike.

"No," she told him, "I'm here on my own. Some people are in trouble over this, and I said I'd try to help out. I thought I'd better see it from the start, is all."

Walter Bengston nodded judiciously. "Way your father would have done it, too. 'See where you are 'fore you try to see where you go,' he always used to say. Smart fella, your father was."

He scowled at the mess the backhoe was making on his grass. In the backhoe's cab Jerry began frowning too, as he tried to remove as much sticky brown earth as possible without putting a crack in the concrete top of James C. Milton's burial vault.

"Hold it," Walter Bengston called. The men from the funeral home stepped forward alertly. They had brought with them a chain-and-pulley device for removing the top from the vault and lifting the casket from the grave hole. Now, after a few moments of concrete-scraping sounds and the metal shrieking of the pulley works, they began rolling the casket on a gurney across the turf.

Walter Bengston turned and put out his hand, his grip as decisive as she remembered, his pale blue eyes shrewd and without guile. "You're looking well, Edwina. Bring your friend over to the house if you like, I'm sure Vivian'll have the coffee on."

Startled, Edwina glanced at McIntyre, with whom she had not communicated by word or look. He was here officially but she was not, and the two of them agreed there was no sense blurring the difference while others were observing.

Walter, however, was gazing not at McIntyre but uphill toward the brick town hall and the old frame school building perched behind it. "Where'd she go? She was watching sharp this way—I thought she was with you."

With a shrug he moved off toward the funeral-home men and the sheaf of papers he was required to sign before the corpse could depart. Edwina stayed behind, by Zebediah Scott's marble stone. Jerry had shut down the backhoe's engine, and the sudden silence was broken only by the labored squeaking of the chain-and-pulley device as it reeled back onto the metal capstan.

A few cars were parked in the freshly tarred lot by the town hall, several more on the older paved patch by the school, now home to the North Branford Historical Society. High on a ladder against the shingle-sided school building, a man was replacing a windowpane.

But whoever the watching woman had been, she was gone.

FOUR

A GOLDEN wash of autumn-afternoon sunlight fell slantingly on the jumbled buildings of Chelsea Memorial Medical Center. Students bearing backpacks, lab techs swinging wire baskets, surgeons in flapping green scrub gowns, and hospital administrators in suits hurried in its narrow streets.

From the ninth floor of the parking garage adjacent to the complex, Edwina looked out over the purposeful bustle to the copper dome of the medical library. Tarnished hazy blue, it rose serenely from the maze's middle, seeming to float on the marble pillars of its portico. Beneath it bits of medical knowledge swarmed like electrons, flowing in steady streams of correction, elaboration, and embellishment from the work going on ceaselessly in stacks and study carrels below.

Or so, Edwina told herself, you like to fancy. Taking the elevator down to the hospital's main entrance she went in past the gift shop and information desk to the house telephone on the wall by the elevators. After using it she proceeded to where the lobby guard stood at his station with his walkie-talkie, his sign-in sheet, and his stock of plastic-encased temporary ID badges.

Signing in and pinning on one of these, she continued past the cafeteria, the X-ray department, and the admitting office to an unmarked stairwell where she climbed three flights, emerging in a utility corridor leading to the newborn intensive care unit.

Here were rows of small green oxygen cylinders, a blood-gas analyzer awaiting repair, a portable respirator for transporting sick infants, and a pair of vacant isolettes. Edwina moved among them, feeling nostalgic—for the overhead page operator's cigarette-roughened voice, for the charred faintly gassy smell of the Bunsen burner in the lab where the interns plated out their Gram-stain specimens—toward telephones ringing, cardiac monitors chirping, IV alarms peeping, and a radio tuned to an easy-listening station.

"Oh, hi, Miss Crusoe," said the secretary, looking up from filing lab slips into charts. Behind her on a bulletin board were thumbtacked perhaps a hundred Polaroids, all of babies looking unimpressed by the amount of fuss being made over them.

"That's last year's graduating class," said the secretary proudly. "Here, let me page Mary Fitzhugh for you."

She pressed a carbon-smudged finger to an intercom button. Past her desk stretched a glass-walled, fluorescent-lit room from whose ceiling dangled heavy-duty extension cords, high-pressure oxygen hoses, and a slowly twirling trio of mobiles in bright primary colors. Beyond on open carts were boxes of disposable diapers, stacks of pink-and-blue blankets, piles of impossibly tiny white cotton jackets, and bottles of sterile water and normal saline, all elbow-

ing for space among sixteen transparent plastic isolettes crammed into a unit meant for ten.

Among the isolettes the nurses moved with practiced ease, alert to the needs of creatures hardly bigger than their hands. No babies were crying in the
room, whose door was propped open by a linen
cart; newborns strong enough to cry were not admitted to a unit where the mere ability to inflate your
own lungs was considered a clinical triumph, and
where the cost of three days' care might top a hundred thousand dollars—assuming, of course, that
you survived three days.

A black-haired woman in tortoiseshell glasses
came to the door and glared through it. "Hello, Edwina, I supposed I'd be hearing from you." She did
not sound as if the prospect were a welcome one.

"Come on," she added, "I can't dilly-dally here.
Put on a gown and scrub up. You're probably
swarming with germs."

"Scrub good," the secretary murmured,
"Fitzhugh's on the warpath again." She returned to
her lab slips with a sigh.

"Sit there," Mary Fitzhugh ordered Edwina when
she had made her way along the narrow aisle between the isolettes, among the scales and suction
bottles, the IV pumps and respirators.

"I leave him with someone else for fifteen minutes," she grumbled as Edwina seated herself on the
metal stool, "and when I come back his A-line's clot-
ted, his alarms are bouncing off the walls, his ventilating pressures are way up and his pulse is way
down—"

The reddened limbs of the infant in the isolette
twitched feebly as Mary flicked its foot, a bit bigger
than a thumbnail, with her gloved index finger. A
stockinette cap covered most of the infant's head,

shielding its eyes from the warming lamps; a gauze dressing was held to its chest with white string ties. Sluggishly its heart rate climbed: seventy-five, eighty.

"Anyway, she's a disaster," Mary Fitzhugh said as she dripped a few cc's of beige formula into the infant's feeding tube. "Professionally, emotionally, financially, and in every other way, Jillian Nash is an utter train wreck."

She looked up, her eyes hostile behind their thick lenses. "I mean, I gather that's what you wanted to ask? Forgive me if you just came by to chat."

"The nursing office called you," Edwina said. It was the nursing director to whom she had spoken from downstairs, to ask permission to visit here. No matter how familiar the hospital still felt to her, she was officially an outsider now and could no more barge in without a by-your-leave than she could enter a foreign country without a visa.

"Listen, Mary," she said, "I know this is probably the last thing you feel like talking about. But—"

"But I'm the only gay woman in this place who's out of the closet," Mary Fitzhugh said, "so you figure I must be an authority on the ones who aren't. Right?"

With impeccable technique she disconnected the baby from its respirator, cleared its breathing tube with a fine plastic catheter, and deftly reconnected it.

"All cats are grey in the dark, huh? So naturally we've got a lot in common. Which is why," Mary went on as the respirator's alarm shrilled and quieted, "now that Jill's on the front page of all the newspapers, I might have troubles of my own. But I don't suppose that occurred to you."

She withdrew her hands from the rubberized

sleeves of the isolette's access ports. Inside, the infant struggled valiantly and mutely.

"People finding excuses not to sit with me at dinner," Mary went on, "looking sideways when they think I'm not looking back. Like you, thinking I must know something about her. But hey, I bought that trip, didn't I? Now I'll have to pay the fare. Again," she finished bitterly. "And so much for honesty's being the best policy. Remember, kid," she added to the infant in the isolette, "you heard it here first."

Edwina got up. "I'm sorry, Mary. It was foolish of me to assume . . . I'm trying to figure this all out, and I just thought you might be able to help, that's all." She turned to go.

"Sit down," Mary Fitzhugh snapped, "you assumed right. I'm just ticked off. I didn't know I'd wind up being gay spokesmodel and information source for the whole damned medical center."

Edwina sat. Mary drew up a thin syringe of orange fluid, a vitamin-C supplement she mixed with more of the beige formula.

"If this kid's gut keeps working," she remarked as she began dripping it in, "I'll go to church for a week."

Edwina said nothing. Mary Fitzhugh was without doubt the sharpest, most dedicated, least intimidatable nurse she had ever met. As head nurse in the newborn unit she confronted slackers, prima donnas, and bumblers of any stripe, from newly hired housemaids to famous neonatal specialists, with one simple rule: do your job or take your gluteus maximus out of here and don't bring it back.

As a result the unit had a higher percentage of graduates—desperately premature babies who lived to have Polaroids taken—than any other newborn facility in the country. Inexperienced interns feared her, second-year residents relied upon her, and attending physicians were divided over whether she ought to have a bronze statue cast of her or a new wing of the medical school dedicated in her honor.

"Anyway," she said, "your long nose has led you to the right place. Again," she added thinly but with a hint of admiration, too; success was something Mary could appreciate.

"Jill Nash had a crush on me five years ago," she continued. "Followed me around, brought me coffee, you know the drill. Boys or girls, at Jillian's level it's the same game, plenty of gimme but not much give. Dumped her life story on me too, which is how I know what a royal mess she was. Still is, I'll bet."

Edwina tipped her head inquiringly.

"Money," Mary said, "was her trouble. She was in hock to her credit cards and I mean deep in it. Bought a car and wrecked it, turned out she hadn't paid insurance. Had a condo foreclosed out from under her, lost a bundle there. The girl just had no idea how to handle cash, I guess because someone else had always done it for her. The IRS was even trying to attach her salary, and you know this place, they'll drop you like a hot rock if that happens. She was an inch from being absolutely on the street."

"So you're telling me," Edwina ventured a cautious smile, "Jill Nash wasn't exactly your idea of an attractive romance prospect?"

Mary Fitzhugh smiled grudgingly back. "'Never lie down,'" she quoted, "'with a woman who's got more troubles than you.' But pretty soon I had my share of troubles, too, because I couldn't get rid of her."

She shook her head, remembering. "Letters, phone calls at all hours, begging me to see her, begging me to tell her what to do. I never encouraged this, Edwina, but she wanted me to come and be her roommate. She thought she was in love, I guess, but I think it was really that she couldn't afford an apartment alone."

"And needed a mother a little bit, maybe?"

Mary nodded. "I suppose, but mostly she was short of bucks. She signed some kind of payment agreement with the IRS, got her loans consolidated with one of those agencies that salvage your burnt-out financial bones—which was funny 'cause her father's a big guy in some big steel conglomerate—but that hardly left her anything to live on. And meanwhile she just got crazier."

She ran the last formula into the feeding tube, backed it up with a ½ cc of sterile water, and capped it. "Finally she came to my place late one night, standing out on the sidewalk shouting. Said she'd kill herself if I didn't let her in."

"I see," said Edwina, giving Jill Nash a mental swat. This was all going to come out in court, every bit of it; if she could find Mary Fitzhugh, so could a prosecutor. And it sounded awful.

"Why do people think that will work, do you suppose?" she thought aloud. "Don't they know you're so heartily sick of them by then, you're ready to throttle them yourself?"

Mary Fitzhugh grimaced her agreement. "Beats me, but that's exactly what I told her. I said her sick obsession made me feel like throwing up, and if she killed herself right outside my door I'd check to be sure she was dead before I called an ambulance."

Edwina stared. "Mary, what if she'd really done it?"

"What if?" Mary demanded. "Why is that supposed to be my problem? I mean, I'd be sorry and all, but responsible for it? No, ma'am, my mother didn't raise any stupid daughters."

She shook her head. "Do what they want, don't do what they don't want, it's nothing but a trap. These helpless people who have no idea what to do and think you've got the secret—you give an inch, next thing you know they've got your checkbook and you're paying for them to get shrunk five times a week or else they'll slit their wrists on you."

She stripped off her plastic gloves. "Anyway, she left and I never heard from her again. I feel sorry for whoever did. The girl's got a vicious streak—I'd stay clean away if I were you."

Edwina got up. "Oh, I don't know. She seems like kind of a sad sack, is all. Just . . . missing something, emotionally."

Mary laughed without amusement as she unsealed a dressing kit. "Right, like maybe everything. Just for instance, when I started backing off from her she sent me a dozen long-stemmed roses. But when I lifted them out of the box all the heads fell off. They'd been hacked off, Edwina, with a knife. And she'd signed the card 'love.'"

"Oh," said Edwina, stunned.

"Yeah, I thought the symbolism was pretty clear myself." Mary moved to the scrub sink, toed the hot water on, and squeezed pHisoHex soap into her hands. Sudsed to the elbows, she turned.

"So keep it in mind is all I'm telling you," she said in a voice that had lost its rancor. "Jill may look helpless but it's all just part of her act. She's about as helpless as a pit viper."

*　　*　　*

Four o'clock was breath-catching time in the wards of Chelsea Memorial Hospital: day shift gone home, fresh coffee in the conference rooms. There the evening-shift staff gathered at Formica tables, mulling over their assignments and updating their patient-care cardexes, planning whose bedbath and linen change had to come first, noting whose visitors were helpful and whose were a pain, and in general plotting how to match too much work to the too-little help available.

Edwina sat at the desk on Seven West, babysitting the call lights and waiting for the telephone to ring while the secretary ran a batch of stat blood work to the chemistry lab. But the phone remained silent and the intercom lights stayed unlit, as even the most demanding patients seemed to know that now was no time of day to need a nurse.

At the other end of the desk, a first-year medical resident frowned irritably over the discharge summary he was writing. Scratching his fountain pen harshly across the page, he scribbled his signature and slapped the finished chart shut with one hand while reaching for the next with the other.

Vipers, Edwina thought troubledly, watching him. But vipers had venom. You knew, if one struck, what was killing you: snake poison.

"William," she said, "can I ask you something?"

The resident waved an impatient hand, not looking up. He wore a rumpled blue shirt, frayed striped tie, navy corduroys, and Hush Puppies. On his belt hung a beeper; the red beeper, she saw, feeling sorry for him.

"Shoot," he said, scribbling faster. When the red beeper went off, your goose was cooked.

"Well, I know this is going to sound strange. But can you think of any circumstances at all under which you would directly"— she lowered her voice and glanced at the intercom to be sure the buttons were all really off —"directly kill a patient?"

"Yes," William Bell replied bitterly, "and I'm living them."

He tossed the chart aside, grabbed for the next. "I need a shower, a shave, clean clothes, some food, and about a year of sleep, none of which I'm going to get. I've been here for thirty hours and I'll be here at least another six, assuming I don't get hit with another unscheduled emergency admission, which I probably will. They're hurting me, Edwina, so what's with the stupid questions?"

But when he turned his smile took the sting out of his tone. William Bell was twenty-seven, with dark curly hair, green eyes, and a look of chronic mischief that even the rigors of internship had not managed to extinguish. He'd been a medical student when Edwina was a staff nurse, and she had liked him a great deal at once while knowing perfectly well that he was too young for her—a fact of which she had taken great pains to convince him.

Will, though, had taken a good deal of convincing; had he been only a bit less a product of his times, she might eventually have given in. After all, to a thirty-five-year-old woman there was little so delightful as an attractive twenty-five-year-old man determinedly engaged in her pursuit.

Two Strindberg tragedies, four Beethoven symphonies, an auction of obscure, privately minted California gold pieces, and a full-scale production of *La Traviata* later, however, William had pronounced himself ready to return to his bachelor apartment, his diet of Tater Tots and frozen pizzas, his Dylan records, monster movies, and full-blast concert tapes of the Rolling Stones; since then they had remained solid friends.

"I'm trying to get my mind around something, that's all," she told him. Then she proceeded to bring him up to speed on the topic of Jill Nash, since if it had not happened to one of his own patients, Will would not have had time to hear about it.

"That's bad, all right," he said when she had finished. "She didn't have an arterial line by any chance? The patient, I mean."

"No," said Edwina, "why?"

He shrugged. "You could shoot air into an A-line, but venous access—you'd have to use a tire pump to kill anybody with that."

"Right," Edwina replied slowly; an air bubble was an interesting idea. "I wonder what other kinds of access you could use, though."

Will turned back to his charts. "Heart-lung bypass, maybe hemodialysis, left-heart-pressure-sensing catheters, angiography probes. Anything where the air could get somewhere and stall the fluid dynamics. Oh, and maybe intrathecal. I don't think air in your spinal fluid would be good for you, either."

"Right," Edwina said resignedly; Berenice Bennington hadn't had any of those things.

He scribbled, frowned, turned to face her again. "But you know what? I've got a feeling you're looking in the wrong place. Pricking of my thumbs, maybe, but—"

Edwina blinked. Will had absorbed his Shakespeare mostly from *Cliffs Notes;* nevertheless, he had caught the drift of it without flaw. From the conference room, nurses began emerging; as if on signal, intercom lights began blinking on too.

"Thing is," he said, "I was kidding before, but if I *were* going to kill someone I sure as heck wouldn't use any drug."

"Because you're a doctor, that's what people would expect?"

Before he could answer his beeper went off shrilly;

at the sound he jumped up, gathering his pen and notebook.

"Right," he said, "but even for a doctor there's drugs you can get and drugs you can't, or not easily, anyway. And to get the second kind you need help, like from a bent pharmacist or a flat-out dope dealer." He stuffed his pen in his shirt pocket and slotted charts hastily into the chart rack.

The pharmacy idea was attractive until one thought about it; a pharmacist could have tainted Mrs. Bennington's Inderal vial. But it was hard to see how a pharmacist could have gotten an emptied pancuronium vial into Jill Nash's pocket. Or how anyone could have; as far as Edwina could tell, no one who'd had such an opportunity had access to the drug.

"So," Edwina said, "either everyone would know you can get the drugs, if they're ones you're allowed to have, or if they're not that kind then some creep you got them from could rat on you."

Will nodded as the returning secretary slid grimly into her swivel chair, punching buttons and dispatching nurse's aides with the speed and authority of an air-traffic controller.

"You're saying maybe I ought to stop wondering about this mysterious other drug Anne Crain thinks had to be there?"

"No," he said, "I'm saying if the pancuronium wasn't fatal, maybe it wasn't meant to be. So—what was it for?"

Diagnosis: reasoning from effect to cause, a sort of reverse process of filling in the blanks. "William, you are wonderful." But he was already sprinting off down the corridor.

Turning back to the nursing desk, she found another man waiting there. "May I help you?" she asked, as the secretary was only goggling at him: at his hair, so thickly oiled it resembled black enamel, at his mustache, waxed and curled like some cartoon villain's, and at his suit, forbidding as an undertaker's.

Altogether he looked like a fellow who foreclosed on family farms, booted orphans and widows out of tenements, and roped helpless damsels to railroad tracks, uttering evil chuckles while engaging in these activities.

He was not, however, chuckling now. "You," he managed in a choked, apoplectic wheeze. "You . . . you dug up my mother!"

* * *

"My card, madam," said Wilbur Freeman when Edwina had calmed him, guided him to the ward's little conference room, poured him a styrofoam cup of coffee which he sniffed and rejected, learned that he preferred to be addressed as "Doctor"—his advanced degrees, he informed her seriously, were in numerology and phrenology—and decided reluctantly that socking him in the jaw would be gratifying but unladylike.

He was, after all, in mourning, which accounted for his dark clothing although not for his similarly hued personality; Wilbur Freeman might or might not be griefstricken, Edwina thought, but he most certainly was a confirmed old sourpuss and a silly one at that. Also, perhaps, a greedy one, a suspicion he confirmed with his very next breath.

"I am," he announced, "ruined. My family name besmirched, my mother's grave desecrated—I tell you, Miss Crusoe, you leave me no recourse but to sue, and to sue most determinedly."

"I see," she replied, glancing at his card, which

informed her in flowery script that he was a personal consultant.

"My clients are elderly ladies," he went on, "of the most immaculate reputation. As was my sainted mother, who passed on so recently." He withdrew a lace-edged handkerchief, touched it theatrically to the corner of one eye.

"My sympathies," Edwina murmured as a smell of mothballs drifted in the air. Wilbur Freeman's fingernails were buffed; his hands were as smooth as a child's and on his left one he sported a diamond pinky-ring.

Its vulgar wink summed him up in an unintended flash. A walker, she realized; he squired rich old ladies around, told their fortunes, and afterward wheedled gifts out of them.

"Indeed," said Wilbur Freeman. "But no sympathy can repair my injury. The stain upon my mother's memory, the very whisper of the horrid word—"

"Murder," said Edwina flatly, wondering when Wilbur Freeman would cut to the chase. "The police think someone murdered her. As you know, the body was exhumed to prove or disprove this, and after the autopsy is completed, your mother will be reburied."

She got up. Threatening to walk away from people often had the effect of loosening their tongues. "As I said, Mr. Freeman, I'm sorry for your loss. I assume legal counsel for you and the other families will handle the hospital's responsibility in this matter, if there is any. Which," she added, "I doubt."

This last was not precisely true. If Jill Nash's past was as checkered as Mary Fitzhugh said, the families' attorneys would claim the hospital should have known she posed a risk. But the bare suggestion that he might not make out like a bandit clearly shook Wilbur Freeman, just as she had intended it to.

"But," she said, "the idea of my having any responsibility in the affair is quite beyond discussion. In point of fact, it is absurd and I think you know that, Mr. Freeman—I'll assume you are not quite such an idiot as you sound right now."

She paused for breath. Her father would have wasted neither words nor anger on such a man, one who so clearly smelled money and wanted only to put his hands on it. But she was not her father, and this fellow had nettled her.

"So why don't you drop this silly story of wounded psychic abilities," she went on with deliberate mercilessness, "or whatever nonsense it is you planned to claim, and tell me what you're really here for. I gather you have a lot of lonely, rich old ladies believing you're Houdini, or some such foolishness. Ladies, perhaps, upon whose generosity you live."

Under this diatribe, Freeman seemed to shrink. "Now," she went on, "I suppose you're afraid that if some sordid scandal comes out, the old ladies' families—most of whom are probably not too nuts about you anyway—will make them drop you."

"You are," said Wilbur Freeman brokenly, "most perceptive. Indeed, you possess abilities which I, in my grief and distress, failed utterly to—"

"Oh, cut it out, Wilbur. I'm a rich girl myself. Don't you think I've run into men like you before? Fast-talking charlatans full of reasons why I ought to hand them bundles of quick cash?"

But at this Wilbur Freeman looked so sincerely stricken, she began against her better judgment to forget her anger and to begin instead feeling sorry for him.

Some tough nut you are, she scolded herself; still, the poor idiot. What in the world could he have been thinking of?

"I mean," she said more gently, seeing that his eyes now really were watery and that the fleshy tip of his nose was reddening ominously, "I do sympathize with you about your mother. It must be dreadful for you, especially now. Did you live with her?"

Wilbur nodded disconsolately. "And it's very . . . it's so . . . I miss her," he managed. "We were quite inseparable, you see. You probably think it's amusing, a grown man and his mother, but—"

Edwina sat down again, seeing the picture clearly in her mind: cups of tea, pieces of toast on little plates.

"No, Wilbur, I don't think it's amusing. But if it's your livelihood that worries you—well, you could start holding séances. Say the spirit of your murdered mother will speak—I'm sure she won't mind; she'd want you to be all right. And you'll have so many clients you won't be able to beat them off with a stick. No family in the world," she added with a smile, "can keep an old lady away from a hot line to the spirit world."

But Wilbur only shook his head. "No, you don't see at all. I've managed this all wrong, Miss Crusoe; I ought to have come to you frankly from the start. I've read things about your work in the newspapers, you see, and when you phoned the nursing director a little while ago I was in her office asking about the—well, about the examination of my mother's remains. I wanted to know just what sort of information might be revealed."

Uh-oh, Edwina thought. "Go on, please."

Freeman looked uncomfortable. "When I heard

your name and realized you must be involved, I'm afraid I—well. I know from my reading also that your family is quite well-fixed financially."

That, she thought, was putting it mildly. But let it go.

"And," he went on, "I'm aware my appearance is unusual. I have been told, cruelly but accurately, I suppose, that even in my normal dress I'm a cross between a dance-hall gigolo and that children's cartoon character . . ."

"Snidely Whiplash?" Edwina said, and wished she hadn't.

Freeman flushed. "At any rate it struck me that I might frighten you with a threat, however baseless, of a lawsuit. You might pay me to go away, if I were obnoxious enough. And—"

"Then," guessed Edwina, "you'd have money enough to go away on. You wouldn't be around when your mother's autopsy showed—but what will it show? What is it you're so afraid of?"

He looked at his hands, clasping and unclasping themselves on the Formica table. "I was with her when she died. She couldn't be alone here, with only strangers to take care of her. They wouldn't know her special needs, you see, they wouldn't—"

Freeman took a deep breath and came to some decision. "Miss Crusoe, my mother was an angel. She loved good music and poetry, gardens and conversation. If a bird struck the parlor window, she wept. But she was also a morphine addict, and at the time of her death I had been administering the drug to her, regularly and without fail, for almost fifteen years."

Edwina nodded. "I see. So when she came in to be treated for pneumonia, you came and stayed with her and supplied her with her drug. How did you obtain it?"

He shook his head. "I'm afraid I can't tell you that. You must know, though, that money makes a great many things possible, and my mother had a lot of it. At one time," he amended. "But the pneumonia was getting better, so much better. The last thing she said to me that night was that she thought she might go home soon."

And so, Edwina thought, she did. "Mr. Freeman, did you give your mother an overdose of morphine the night she died?"

Freeman looked appalled. "Oh, no. Heavens, no, I was most careful as always. I even looked up all her other medicines, to prevent untoward reactions."

"I see. How commendable. And as far as you know she wasn't getting any drug that would increase morphine's effect?" This of course could be checked, but she wondered how thorough he had been about it.

"None," he said seriously. "A vitamin syrup she swallowed, horrid stuff, I mixed it in applesauce for her. Erythromycin, an antibiotic in her intravenous. It would have been penicillin but she was allergic to that. And cortisone cream for a little itchy rash she had—her skin was very sensitive. None of those drugs interact with morphine, as far as I could learn. And I was most meticulous in my research."

Quite right, she thought, eyeing him with new respect. "And she'd never reacted badly to morphine before?"

Freeman shook his head sadly. "Only to its absence. Miss Crusoe, until this other matter came up I believed my mother's death was natural. She was very old, that's all. When I woke up and found her gone I thought she'd simply . . . slipped away."

He looked up and saw her expression. "When I said I stayed with her," he explained, "I meant all the time. She wasn't used to other people doing things. Taking her to the . . . toilet," he pronounced the word with shy difficulty, "things of that nature. I slept nights in a chair, in her room with her. She said having me there made her feel not so afraid."

A sudden unwished-for picture of her own mother came into Edwina's mind: brisk, busy, and indomitable, Harriet Crusoe was the prolific and madly popular writer of romance novels that sold in the millions. At seventy-four she seemed in her flowered silk dresses and masses of pearls quite likely to go on forever.

Or so, Edwina thought with a thump of premonitory sorrow, you like to fancy. "Go on, please," she told Freeman gently.

He nodded, gave his handkerchief a long, honking blow. "That night I'd put her to bed at ten-thirty, as usual. I worked for a while—I'm writing a book, you see, on the astral cosmology of . . . well, never mind. At midnight I turned out the light and settled in. The nurses had given me a blanket and a pillow—"

Considering the work of which his presence relieved them, Edwina thought, they might at least have offered him a cot.

"—and I went to sleep. I sleep lightly as a rule, but I was tired. The strain of my mother's illness took its toll, of course, and then too I was always anxious over—"

"Being caught injecting her," Edwina finished for him. "It must have been horribly nerve-wracking."

He frowned. "Quite so. At any rate I barely

stirred when the night nurse came in with Mother's antibiotic dose. That must have been two A.M. or so. Shortly afterwards, though, I awoke."

"How shortly?" So far, his tale agreed entirely with what Edwina already knew: Jill Nash had given Elinor Freeman a dose of erythromycin right on schedule, at two o'clock in the morning.

"Two-thirty-two by my mother's travel clock," he replied. "They glow, you know. Radium. I'll never forget those glowing green numerals, and the silence. I thought I'd heard something, and then I realized what I heard was her not breathing."

"Did you call for help?" she asked.

Freeman shook his head. "No. I took her hand, her skin was cool, and I knew she was gone, so I went to the nursing station and told them. It was too late for any measures, I felt certain, not that she would have wanted them."

"The grace of a happy death," said Edwina.

He looked up gratefully. "Yes. I must comfort myself with that. But Miss Crusoe, what is going to happen to me? Will I go to jail? I'm afraid I'm rather a coward about many things."

But not about the ones that count, Edwina thought acutely, having in the past twenty minutes entirely revised her opinion of this unusual gentleman.

"I don't know," she told him honestly, "but I do think you ought to go right now and talk to a friend of mine."

McIntyre would know how to handle this. Confession after all might be good for the soul, but it could be rather bad for one's legal situation. A confidential word in the district attorney's ear might smooth Freeman's way considerably, assuming it could be smoothed at all.

She scribbled the number on a lab slip. "Here. Don't say a word of what you've told me, and for heaven's sake don't say I sent you. Simply tell him that you have information to give, but you must speak with legal counsel before giving it. I'll let the medical examiner's people know about the morphine they'll find."

She folded the slip, handed it to him. "But I must say, Mr. Freeman, you are in great trouble here. I'm sure a lawyer would tell you to speak of this only with your own private attorney. Especially," she added, "if the autopsy shows your mother died of morphine. Or—" Another thought struck her. "—if financial considerations . . . that is, regarding your future expectations . . ."

But he was already rejecting this. "I am, Miss Crusoe, a most experienced drug giver. Had she received too large a dose I would have noticed at once, as you being a nurse must know."

Right again. Immediate cardiac standstill for way too much, swift onset of respiratory depression for lesser amounts of the drug. Surely he would have noticed. Death by morphine overdose, if Wilbur Freeman's story could be believed, and she thought it could, was in this case very unlikely.

"As for a motive," he went on, "did I kill my mother for her money? I fear the idea would be humorous if it were not, to me, so tragic." He got up: a tall, pale man with a face like a cruel joke and a heart as pure as Little Nell's. Edwina hoped it would give him the strength of ten, for surely he would need it soon.

"I admit the idea of financial gain occurred to me, but from the hospital, after I heard about the other deaths and learned my mother's might have been one of them. Not from her estate."

Edwina looked up at him, amazed. "You mean after all that care you took of her, you aren't her beneficiary?"

He laughed sadly. "Oh, indeed I am. Of her house, which just now needs a new roof, replacement of the furnace, plumbing and wiring repairs, and the extermination of mice, squirrels, and bats as well as quite a large and flourishing termite colony."

She began to understand. "But no actual money. Nothing you can live on. That's why you're worried about scandal."

He spread his hands in agreement. "My mother was a wealthy woman once, Miss Crusoe. But in keeping her supplied with her drug, I spent all she had. I may be forced to think of holding those séances, unless the state takes on the task of maintaining me. While," he added, "it is confining me, if it comes to that."

He put on his hat, an old black homburg that made him look wickeder. "Thank you for listening," he said, "I shan't trouble you again."

In parting he raised her hand briefly and startlingly to his lips, which were dry and papery as moth wings.

FIVE

"HELLO, darling, what a lovely surprise," said Harriet Crusoe in the plummy British accents that, over years of adopting them for her public appearances, had found their way also into her private speech habits.

Americans, she maintained, adored ersatz royalty principally because they had been so long unburdened by the real kind that they had forgotten what a pain it was. And why not indulge them, she argued, in their upper-crust fantasies? After all, she never claimed to be more than distant cousins with Elizabeth, which in fact she was, and besides it sold books like hotcakes.

"Hello, Mother," said Edwina, a little breathless as always at coming home again.

The Crusoe house stood at the end of a long, curving drive that wound between ancient maple trees, their branches here in the Litchfield hills bare against a night sky. Two granite lions guarded the entrance to the inner compound, which with the main house consisted of barns, stables, garages, guest cottages, the greenhouses, a conservatory, a riding ring, and servants' quarters.

As Edwina pulled up in the Fiat Spyder, an ancient Italian two-seater convertible whose acronym—Fix It Again, Tony—might have been amusing were it not quite so accurate, an old man in a navy peacoat and black watch cap stepped alertly from a side door of the big house.

Greeting her with real affection, Watkins took charge with practiced ease not only of the pampered sports car but also of her bags and the carrying-cage from which Maxie was loudly protesting his confinement.

"Give 'er a polish while she's 'ere, Miss?" Watkins asked, patting the fender while aiming a confidential glance at Maxie, now hunkering in his cage and awaiting the indulgences to come.

"Yes, thanks," Edwina said, gazing up at the many lighted windows of the house. "And could you look at the timing belt? I know it's not your job, but no one in the shop is as good with it as you are, Mr. Watkins."

"Glad to, Miss," he replied, seating himself with pleasure behind the leather steering wheel. "Rubber timin' belt," he said indulgently. "Them Eye-talians is awful optimists, ain't they? Sure do build pretty autos, though." Dropping the little Fiat into first gear he roared off in the direction of the garages.

Now in a rustle of flowered silks, Harriet Crusoe rose from the settee where she was writing—in longhand, with a fountain pen—the next of her fabulously suspenseful, immensely popular romance novels. Scented with Pear's soap and Joy perfume, she embraced Edwina warmly and peered past her to the entry hall.

"Has he come with you, dear?" she asked with a faint frown, as if suspecting Martin McIntyre might have hidden himself behind the coat tree, or perhaps in the elephant-leg umbrella stand.

"No, Mother," Edwina said, "Martin is working. Besides, he knows you disapprove."

Harriet's eyes widened. "Surely I've never said or implied such a thing to him."

Smiling inwardly, Edwina crossed the small, snug parlor to the fire on the blue-and-white tile-faced hearth, each antique tile depicting a different fairy-tale scene. As a child she had never tired of these: Rapunzel with her golden hair, the frog-prince in his tiny crown, and a boy astride the back of a great white flying goose, its wings magnificently spread, whose story she had never been able to discover.

"You don't have to, Mother," she said, "he's a detective. Besides, it comes off you in visible waves whenever you see him. But I didn't come up here to talk about that, you know."

On a tray by the fireplace Harriet's evening snack had been laid out: wheatmeal biscuits and green tea. Sighing, she sat before it and poured out two steaming cups from the china pot.

"Darling, I say this to you now as a mother and a friend. No good ever comes of associating beneath one's station. I know that must sound horridly undemocratic, but when you are as old as I am you will see that it is true."

Edwina sat across from her mother, accepted tea. "Sounds to me like an argument for dying young. Besides, in your books the heroines are always in love with unsuitable men—pirates and highwaymen and disgraced younger sons. In *Talley's Folly* the love-interest was a London grave-robber, for heaven's sake."

A look of reminiscent pleasure lit Harriet's face. "He was also," she pointed out, "a surgeon. And my lovers aren't obliged to live happily ever after—only until page three-twenty-five, or thereabouts."

Edwina munched a wheatmeal biscuit. In her mother's world police officers parked at the service gate and came in by the kitchen, in the unhappy event they ever visited the house at all—public servants, to be sure, but servants nevertheless. And however personable they might be, one did not befriend servants; it only confused them and made them discontented with their lot.

"But never mind," said Harriet. "You must learn your own lessons. At least he's not a fortune hunter."

"And how do you know that?" In Harriet's romances, fortune hunters were the lowest form of life and always came to ghastly, well-deserved, and lusciously described ends.

"My dear," replied Harriet, "you forget I've met him. I won't deny he has a certain rakish charm. And I, who can hear a cash register ringing in a man's mind at two hundred paces, have not heard one ringing in his."

She set down her cup. "More to the point, I've seen you two together. If he wanted your money he would be spending it right now. You are not wise in love, Edwina, only lucky."

"Surely," Edwina parried lightly, "good luck must count for something?"

Harriet paused, a biscuit halfway to her lips. "I didn't say it was good luck, dear. Now where is that rascal Maxie, and what was it you did come all this way to talk about?"

"Watkins took him to the kitchen," said Edwina, wondering whether to be relieved at the change of subject or disturbed at the note on which it had occurred. The former, she decided.

"Probably," she said, "he's out there feeding him pheasant tongues, or something." Maxie always returned from Litchfield with his taste for exotic victuals thoroughly piqued; the country diet of live mice, table scraps, and treats met very well his standards of feline cuisine—although, alas, not quite so well with his digestion, which was why he was confined to the kitchen.

Edwina shrugged mentally; everyone deserved a fling now and then. But as this thought came dangerously near her mother's idea of her own present romantic circumstances, she smiled and changed the subject yet again.

"I wanted," she sat forward, "your advice."

Harriet's eyebrows rose with amusement and poorly concealed skepticism. "Really," she drawled. Smiling in a way Edwina recognized only too well, she played with the rope of perfect, perfectly enormous pearls that were her public trademark. "And upon what subject, pray," she asked, "may I enlighten you?"

"The subject," said Edwina, "is murder."

She watched as her mother's eyelids lowered shrewdly and with interest. "By methods," she continued, "and for reasons unknown, although motives and methods have both been suggested by physical evidence and persons acquainted with the suspect."

Harriet made a face of unconcealed distaste. "By persons acquainted I suppose you mean friends, betraying the suspect's secrets? My, how important it must have made them feel, giving information to the police. Almost," she added in astringent tones, "like being on television."

Edwina coughed delicately. "Yes, well. Actually the friend was speaking to me, which I hardly regard as a betrayal."

Harriet fixed her daughter in her penetrating gaze. "You are very like your father," she said in a voice that had lost all affectation. In the firelight's leaping glow, her face was like some ancient sibyl's: cruel and wise.

"Yes, I suppose that's true," Edwina said. "But you encouraged it, you know. If what you wanted was a Junior League candidate, Mother, you should have raised me up to be one instead of letting Dad make me learn to ride the meanest mounts in the stable."

"The Junior League is the meanest mount in the stable," said Harriet with a smile. "But go on, now, with the thread of this tangled skein you've brought me."

"Yes." Edwina sat straight. "Three unrelated hospital patients have died unexpectedly under the care of one nurse, who was found after the third death to have an empty vial of a deadly substance in her pocket. Traces of the stuff were found at autopsy in the body of the third victim, but there remains some question as to whether it was the actual cause of death."

"And the other two?" asked Harriet with a fine sense of the pertinent.

"The results of their postmortem exams are not yet known. One will show morphine, but I think not a fatal amount, given secretly by a relative without any motive for killing her."

"Relatives," Harriet put in darkly, "always have motives."

"Fine," Edwina conceded, "but this one's heart is broken. No relative at all was present at the death of

James Milton, the second victim; no one went near him but the nurse. In the third case a niece was present, but as she was the one who raised the alarm I find her difficult to suspect. I know nothing of their relationship, but if she wished her aunt's death to be certain, she should not have screamed for help—and anyway, the timing and method are wrong for her to have been involved."

Harriet had taken up her fountain pen. Now she glanced up from the lines of black ink script she was making on a yellow legal pad. "And the nurse? What motive had she for doing such dreadful deeds?"

"Thwarted love," Edwina replied sadly. "She's immature, a blaming sort of girl, with a strong and parasitic attachment to another woman. And . . . manipulative. The type who thinks she can make people feel the way she wants them to feel, perhaps by . . ."

"By offering up sacrifices," Harriet finished for her. "A mistake in any case, as the careful student of history may learn, especially as it is always so much more difficult to sacrifice oneself for others, rather than others for oneself. She meant, I gather, to prove her love? Or so the theory goes," she added in tones of deep disapproval.

"That's the theory so far," agreed Edwina. "She denies all, of course. But her friend is very worried, especially as this is not the first time the nurse has been accused of—"

Harriet looked up sharply. "Not the first time?"

Briefly, Edwina described the notes Jill Nash had received from Millie Clemens, whose husband's death had by all accounts been a natural one despite its having occurred under Jill's care.

"No," pronounced Harriet decisively when she

had heard this. "I don't believe it for a moment. That's much too convenient—there must be some connection."

"Now, Mother, just because it wouldn't work for one of your romances doesn't mean that it couldn't be—"

"Did Jill Nash tell her friend?" Harriet demanded. "Did she say, 'See here, I've killed for you, now you must love me'?"

"No, she didn't tell anyone. But she did say she *would*—"

Harriet looked impatient. "Not the same at all. She's not frankly mad, I gather—not trying to summon up occult powers or appease diabolical beings, or any such foolishness as that?"

"No," Edwina said slowly again, beginning to see what her mother was driving at.

"Well, then," said Harriet, "how did she expect to impress anyone? Assuming you haven't a practical motive like eliminating a rival or inheriting a fortune, what's the point of killing for love if the beloved isn't made aware of it?"

Edwina frowned. "I hadn't thought of that."

"No, dear, of course not, because you haven't a manipulative bone in your body. Which I regard as a handicap, by the way, but let it pass. Meanwhile, involvement with all the victims and an empty poison vial discovered in one's pocket—the combination rather outweighs any little confusion in the motives department, I must say. Things are indeed looking rather bad for the nurse."

She looked thoughtful. "But it's this Clemens person who interests me," she went on, "since she has a motive one can actually believe in—revenge. She thinks this nurse killed her husband, but no one takes her seriously, is that it?"

"Yes, because it's not true. He wasn't murdered."

"That," Harriet replied, "is both tremendously unlikely and entirely beside the point."

"Mother," Edwina protested, as peeking at the pad on which Harriet had been writing she saw three chapters of yet another new novel already well sketched out, and the skeleton present for a fourth. "I came for some practical help here, not to supply you with plot twists for your next blockbuster."

"The point *is*," Harriet went on imperturbably, her hand moving steadily over the page, "that Mrs. Clemens *believes* her husband was murdered, and believes also that the culprit will go unpunished unless she herself arranges punishment. After all, it hardly matters which murder the nurse is punished *for*, does it? And to be sure she's punished for one, let's make her guilty of several of them. That," she finished a line with a flourish, "is how I would approach the situation."

"No," Edwina insisted, "it may be neat, motive-wise, but you overlook one important thing. How would she do it? Assuming she decided to kill three people and make Jill look guilty, which if you ask me is pretty byzantine right there, how could she arrange it?"

"Where there's a will, dear," Harriet Crusoe murmured. "But you're right. Likely the whole thing is too complex for a nonmedical character to do. I shall have to rethink that part of it."

"Wonderful," said Edwina. "Meanwhile I don't imagine you have any nonliterary suggestions to offer? Ones I might be able to use in what we laughingly call real life?"

Harriet considered. "No," she said finally, "I don't. Just bumble along as you have been until you find out something, is all I can advise."

She got up, seized the poker from among the fire tools and jabbed at the log now falling to embers on the hearth. "I will say this much, though. Someone should speak with this Clemens woman again."

Edwina sighed. "Mother, she's bereaved, maybe a little unhinged. But her husband's death didn't even happen on the same ward as these other occurrences. The Nash girl was only pulled there for one night because the other floor was busy and her own floor's census was low. There was no way Jill could have known that in advance, and I hardly think these killings were done on the spur of the moment. The method, whatever it is, is simply so devious as to require some preparation. Meanwhile . . ."

Really, it was too bad of Harriet to seize on such an unlikely idea this way. Edwina had hoped her mother might help clarify her thoughts, not jumble them further with all this unuseful speculation.

"Yes, go on," Harriet invited.

Edwina controlled her impatience. "The Clemens man was autopsied, and there was absolutely no evidence of anything but a coronary attack. So," she finished, "if I talk to Millie Clemens now it will just upset her all over again, when she's only involved in the first place on account of an unfortunate coincidence."

"Indeed." Harriet wielded the fire tongs to place a split beech log on the andirons. "And is it coincidence that she began accusing Jill Nash of murder days before anyone else did?" She turned. "Really, dear, all else aside, doesn't that one point suggest a rather unusual degree of prescience to you?"

Edwina sighed. As usual, her mother had waited for the whole house of cards to be constructed before demolishing it with a fingertip. "You're right," she admitted. "It's implausible."

Harriet replaced the tongs in their polished brass stand, dusting her hands with pleasure at a task well performed. "I so enjoy doing for myself," she remarked as the new wood blazed up.

Repressing a smile—Harriet's idea of doing for herself included burning but not cutting, splitting, stacking, or hauling wood, nor sweeping ashes from the hearth afterward—Edwina allowed as how self-sufficiency was indeed fulfilling.

"At any rate," said Harriet, returning to her chair, "there is vastly more to Mrs. Clemens than meets the eye, I assure you."

"So you think I ought to go and see her?" Edwina groaned inwardly at the prospect; having had a taste of Millie Clemens's epistolary style, she found the thought of meeting the venomous letter-writer an enormously unpleasant one.

"Oh, yes," replied Harriet, "I do. In fact, based on what you've just told me, I believe you might be wise to do it rather soon, dear."

A frown flitted momentarily across her face. "Before," she finished, "someone else does."

*   *   *

After midnight, tucked up in her warmest robe, Edwina sat by the window in her old room watching the season's first snow sift out of the sky, dry white grains whispering in the bay laurel and rhododendron bushes massed against the house.

"Harriet thinks you're probably not after my money," she said into the telephone.

McIntyre chuckled. She could almost see him in his battered tweed recliner: a seltzer and lime in one hand, *New York Post* folded open to the sports pages in the other.

"Progress," he said. "Don't worry, she'll come around. Did she mention my rakish charm again?"

Edwina laughed as Maxie shifted in her arms; half an hour earlier she had slipped down the back stairway to the kitchen and found him there, waiting for her with perfect confidence. Now he slept with one black velvet paw extended, dreaming no doubt of the enormous barn rodents he would capture and devour tomorrow.

"No one," she assured McIntyre, "ever fails to mention that. How," she added cautiously, "are things going?"

"All right." She heard him drop the newspaper. "Slow, as usual. The autopsy reports are in, and they're not particularly enlightening."

She sat up. "Really. Why?"

"Well, first of all, the Bennington woman is iffy."

"Because Anne Crain won't say she died of pancuronium." Of course; all exhumed bodies were autopsied by the state's chief medical examiner, and the remains of James Milton and Elinor Freeman would have been transported to the state laboratory for this procedure.

But Berenice Bennington had gone straight to Chelsea's own morgue, and although Anne as a deputy examiner was empowered to perform such examinations, she was—as she had said herself—not about to rubber-stamp one.

"You've got it," said McIntyre. "Meanwhile, I had a visitor today, a Wilbur Freeman. He felt I'd lend a sympathetic ear to a story he had to tell. You have any idea where he got that notion?"

Outside, the snow was thickening now to fat white flakes. "I can't imagine," said Edwina.

"Right," said McIntyre, undeceived. "Well, his story was interesting partly because I already had the autopsy findings on my desk. Mrs. Freeman, as it turns out, died from something called anaphylactic shock, which my medical dictionary tells me is a big—and I mean really big—allergic reaction."

"Yes, really big. And fast. Not morphine, then."

"Nope. Which makes Freeman a dimwit but nothing much worse. It was Milton who died of morphine. Lots of morphine, none of which he was supposed to get for the simple reason that—"

"He was allergic to it," Edwina said. She sank back against the cushions of the window seat.

"Right again. Did you know that, or did you guess?"

"Guessed," she said, "it just balances out so well. And I'll venture another one: Elinor Freeman got an unordered dose of penicillin, the night she died."

"Very nice. Actually, we don't have that cut and dried, but according to the allergist's skin tests in her medical records, it was the only thing she was allergic to. So enlighten a tired old cop: drugs don't come out of a common jug anymore, do they? That is, the ward's medication room doesn't have a big bottle of morphine and another one of penicillin—"

"No. Drugs come in what's called unit doses now, already prepared and with the patient's name on them. If you work the evening shift, for example, and on your time you need to give three doses of a certain drug to patient X, the pharmacy sends them up to you already mixed and labelled, and anything you don't use goes back and gets credited to the patient's account."

"Uh-huh," he said. "So tell me, where did these extra doses come from?"

Extra morphine for James Milton, spare penicillin for Elinor Freeman, pancuronium—and something else?—for the Bennington woman.

Edwina gazed at the cut-crystal lamp by her bed. The carpet it shone on was antique handloomed Tabriz, the bedstead's canopy Belgian linen, the bed itself built of bird's-eye maple cut before the Boston Tea Party. At the moment she would happily have traded them all for a half-share in one battered tweed recliner.

"All right," she said slowly, "try this. You don't give one morphine dose. You substitute sterile water, or skip the dose altogether. But you don't send it back, either. You squirt it out into a medicine cup and later you draw it up into a different syringe. You hide the syringe in your locker, maybe."

"Do that a couple of times, you've got a big jolt of morphine stored away."

"Right," she said, "and the same for the penicillin. All you have to do, see, is come out even, dose for dose—nothing missing, nothing left over. And make sure no one sees you doing it. That's how addicted nurses get their drugs."

"And the other stuff, the pancuronium?"

"That's a bit more difficult, but not impossible—generally the anesthesia resident brings it to the floor if it's needed, and forgets whatever's left over. It gets stuck in the medication room refrigerator and after a while it gets tossed out."

"Or picked up by someone who wants some, who can get into the med-room refrigerator."

"In the unlikely event someone does want it. There's no buzz from it; it just locks your muscles up. Meanwhile, I assume you know about the letters from the Clemens woman? Harriet got very hot on them when I told her; she's sure Mrs. Clemens is involved."

He did know about them, but he didn't agree with Harriet. "I'll be following up," he said, "but don't expect much. It is a funny thing about Mrs. Clemens, but Jill Nash is still the only one who could get at all the victims, all the drugs, and has a motive besides."

"If you call killing for love but not telling the loved one about it a motive," she reminded him.

"Right, which I wouldn't if Jill weren't such a weird duck. But she is, Edwina. You don't need to be a psychiatrist to see there's something wrong about her, and I don't mean her living arrangements or her love life."

"I suppose," Edwina sighed. "It's really more Harriet who's stuck on the Clemens thing than I am. I guess maybe Mrs. Clemens sniffed out something strange about Jill's personality, which I agree, it wouldn't take Freud to do, and when her husband died she put two and two together and got five. Right in theory but all wrong in practice, if you see what I mean."

"Maybe," McIntyre said. "What is clear is, nobody killed Walt Clemens. I saw his autopsy report too, and the guy had a clot the size of a Studebaker in one of his coronary arteries."

"Okay," Edwina conceded, "so Harriet's wrong. But it's still darned odd for Jill Nash to start commiting murders *after* someone starts suspecting her, and so is the switch in method. Why would she switch to a drug that's not certain to be fatal? Which if Anne Crain says it wasn't, then maybe it wasn't. And why do it at all when a wide-awake witness who's sure to call for help so your victim might not even die, and also sure to accuse you of a medication error at the very least—why do it when the witness is sitting right smack-dab in the room with you?"

"Your problem," said McIntyre, "is that you expect murderers to be reasonable, when if they were reasonable they wouldn't be murderers in the first place."

"And your problem," she shot back, "is that your

job has gotten you so used to an atmosphere of moral chaos, it's starting to corrupt your logic."

McIntyre laughed, and the conversation shifted to a series of inquiries, cautions, and admonishments having to do with one another's health and welfare: the taking of vitamins, the wearing of enough warm clothes, and the avoiding of dangers ranging from road hazards (mostly in Edwina's case) to desperate criminals equipped with large-caliber weapons (mostly in McIntyre's) until finally, reluctantly, they said good night.

Sighing, Edwina climbed into bed and lay there frowning as Maxie crept stealthily to settle in the crook of her arm.

"I don't get it," she told him. "Jill looks guilty as hell, I'll admit that. But why do it *when* she did— with a witness there? That's the thing that just doesn't make sense to me. I mean, even unreasonable murderers don't *want* to get caught."

Maxie yawned as if to say barn mice didn't want to get caught, either, but that didn't stop him from pursuing them whenever he got an opportunity. And as he planned on getting one quite early in the morning, couldn't she please settle down so he could also get some rest?

Edwina sat up straight. Opportunity: not only to kill, but to make sure Jill Nash took the blame—for which a witness came in mighty handy, didn't it?

"Heavens, Max, how could I have missed that?"

Maxie opened one eye balefully, his brief look answering her question with animal bluntness.

"You don't," she told him, "have to be snide about it."

Then, satisfied, she snapped off the bedside lamp. Nothing more could be done tonight, but tomorrow was most emphatically another day—a day during which she would do a little pursuing of her own.

* * *

Tomorrow, Millie Clemens thought confidently.

She had mailed the letters off early. Surely it would take no more than a single day to deliver them, since none was going more than a few towns distant from her own. Tomorrow, surely, she would hear from someone like herself: lonely, grieving, and furious.

Thinking this she switched off the living-room lamps, made her way to the kitchen, and began fixing a cup of tea.

Never mind those knock-out drops of Hiram's; that stuff, as Walter would have put it—if he were alive, which he was *not*, Millie thought, grabbing a saucepan and giving the faucet knob a vicious twist, and we all knew whose fault *that* was, didn't we?— that stuff was strong enough to drop-kick you into the next county, and left you headachy and groggy all the next day.

Although some nights it was worth it to be whisked off to a place where there were no dreams, only absolute nothingness. Once you took the drops, for a few hours it was as if you did not exist. Which she supposed was exactly what Hiram had intended, and on some nights it was just fine with Millie, too.

But not on this one. Setting the water on the gas-ring she found her used teabag, limp but serviceable, sitting in its saucer. Plopping the bag into her cup, she thought that tonight she would drink her tea, sleep sweetly, and wake up early in the morning all bright-eyed and bushy-tailed, because it would be—*tomorrow*.

And tomorrow it would all begin happening.

SIX

I T is not the thought that counts, Edwina reminded herself the next morning; it's the action that counts, and so she need not feel guilty about wishing to thump Ted B. Nash's head against some unyielding surface, firmly and repeatedly, until some sense began sinking into it.

Cradling the car phone between her shoulder and chin while negotiating a particularly tricky S-curve, she listened with one ear while monitoring the Fiat's engine sounds with the other. Meanwhile Ted Nash blithered on about progress, results, and the kind of value he expected to get for the kind of money he was paying her, dammit.

Last night's snow was almost all already melted, only a few pale patches remaining beneath the big old spruces lining the narrow road. Snarling, the little Fiat sped tightly through the turns and attacked the upgrades with gusto; Mr. Wilkins had done a good job on it.

Ted B. Nash paused for breath, which was surprising as he apparently had the lung capacity of a sperm whale.

"What is it you actually do for that big steel company you work for?" she asked him, downshifting through a crossroads and past a small white sign announcing the Deptford Village Limits.

"I'm CEO, worldwide advertising and public relations," he replied tightly. "What does that have to do with anything?"

Edwina slowed further, entering the village which consisted of a general store, three gas pumps, a post office, and a small rundown frame building with a sloping front porch and a sign that said Hawkins Real Estate.

The building's windows were shuttered, its parking lot empty and a padlock dangling forlornly from its door. The town of Deptford did not seem to be experiencing a land boom—or any other kind of boom, either.

"It means," she told Ted B. Nash, "I can put what I know so far in a way you'll be sure to understand."

Pulling up in front of the store, she shut the Fiat's engine off and spoke firmly and clearly into the car phone's handset.

"Just for starters," she said, "your daughter isn't going to be doing endorsements for any nationally advertised, name-brand accounts any time real soon. Not until One-a-Day comes out with their new, improved multiple vitamins plus strychnine, or maybe when the folks who make electric chairs decide to do a demo tape."

She pulled a map from the glove compartment. "That's the kind of fame Jill's picking up around here, you see, not only with the newspapers but also with the police, who I happen to know think they've got her cold, or as good as. They're making a list and checking it twice, naturally, but she's the only one on it and I'm the only one even thinking of looking for anyone else. Are you reading me here, Ted? Am I getting through to you?"

"That bad," he said quietly after a moment. "My attorneys, though, are assuring me that—"

"They can get the charges bargained down to manslaughter, maybe negligent homicide? Three counts, that's fifteen to forty years by my reckoning. If they can do it, which if I were you I wouldn't bet the farm on."

She snapped the map flat. "But listen, if that's the kind of outcome you'll be happy with, Ted, then maybe you should—"

"No," he broke in, "no, I want you to keep on. I guess I'm just too used to getting all my news from yes-men, and I wish I weren't beginning to wonder myself if maybe she might be—"

"Guilty? That's good, because that's what I'm wondering, too, and if I'm not mistaken it's what you hired me to find out. I'm glad we still understand each other."

Scanning the map, she switched the Fiat's ignition back on. "So today, with your permission, I'm going to stand on doorsteps offering sincere condolences on your behalf to the relatives of your daughter's victims."

Ted B. Nash spluttered wordlessly.

"That way," she said, "there's just a bare chance they'll invite me in, and maybe I can find out what cooks. If anything. It's a long shot, but I don't quite see what other choice there is except breaking and entering, and I don't do that sort of work."

She stuck the map back in the Fiat's glove compartment. "Not even," she added, "for the kind of money you're paying me, which I don't need and which you're not far from having handed back to you."

"You're a hard woman, Miss Crusoe," Ted Nash conceded grudgingly.

"Yes, I suppose I am," Edwina replied. "But then, it's a hard world, isn't it, Mr. Nash?"

As, she thought, you are only beginning to learn; if those lawyers of yours are telling you anything hopeful at all then you're being flim-flammed, or they are.

"I'll let you know what I find out," she finished, and broke the connection before Ted B. Nash could start blithering again.

*   *   *

The *New Haven Register*'s obituary column listed Berenice Bennington's address as Poole Road, just outside Deptford. On Edwina's map this road was shown as dirt-surfaced, primitive but apparently passable.

Actual firsthand experience of Poole Road, however, revealed some major understatement—either that, Edwina thought, gritting her teeth as she negotiated the washboard-textured track, or considerable actual malice—on the part of the mapmaker, who probably thought the badlands of North Dakota were a little primitive, too.

At length a small wooden sign promised Poole Farm, One Mile. Hoping this sign had not been placed by the mapmaker, whose sense of distance now also began to seem suspect, she downshifted yet again and continued urging the Fiat uphill between long-abandoned pastures overgrown solidly into bramble thickets.

Finally the road leveled out and began to widen; pea gravel pinged hopefully against the car's underside as the thickets were replaced first by newish-looking barbed wire strung between straight, well-maintained fenceposts, then by white pickets and a neatly mown lawn.

The road became pavement and a few feet later was blocked by a gate whose sign read No Entry—Private. As Edwina stopped the car and got out—she had, she realized, somehow approached the house by a disused rear driveway; if the gate was locked she would have to go all the way back to the main road, then try again to find her way to a front entrance—she heard something that sounded like but of course could not be the Hound of the Baskervilles, baying bloodthirstily and coming closer fast.

Her first thought upon turning and actually seeing the thing was that McIntyre was right: road hazards were indeed the danger she had most to worry about, and this dog definitely qualified as one. Hitting it with anything less than an eighteen-wheeler was certain to be fatal, although probably not to it; the creature looked massive enough to stop a locomotive without suffering much more than a few superficial scratches.

"Nice doggie," she croaked, whereupon the animal skidded to a halt, pea gravel flying. It was not the Hound after all, merely the biggest Doberman she had ever seen.

Also perhaps the prettiest: more red than black, its ears and tail uncropped—a fact that gave Edwina, now that she had not been devoured on the spot, some measure of hope. Chopping off a dog's ears and tail in conformance to fashion seemed the grossest sort of barbarism, nor was she surprised that breeds suffering such savagery shared also a penchant for irritableness. This dog's look was more curious than hostile, although Edwina was not yet tempted to make any sudden moves. "Nice dog," she tried, at which the monstrous beast wriggled happily.

"Good girl," she said, extending her hand palm down, fingers curled. As if on signal the enormous dog sprang at her, slamming its massive flank against her hip and nearly bowling her over in its joy at having made a new human friend.

"Woof," laughed Edwina, smoothing back the silky ears and struggling to keep her feet. "What are you doing out here, girl? Aren't you supposed to be inside the fence? Come on, now, I like you but you're getting me all messed up. Sit, girl. Sit."

Freezing in mid-wriggle the dog obeyed: head high and spine stiff, it sat in an attitude of military attention. Then slowly it offered up its big, black-toenailed paw.

"Well, aren't you a wonder," said Edwina. She was about to try finding out what other commands the dog knew when footsteps sounded in the pea gravel. Rapid footsteps; angry footsteps—human footsteps. Quietly the dog lay down and covered its muzzle.

"Ruby," said Mrs. Bennington's niece, "you naughty girl." Kneeling to slip a collar around the dog's neck, she snapped a red leather leash to it. "I've been hunting you all morning."

She looked up at Edwina. "This road is private," she began, "you'll have to—oh. I remember you; what are you doing here?"

She was wearing a blue denim jacket, red sweater, snug jeans and a most unwelcoming expression. In the crisp pleasant morning her pretty face was pinched with cold and with irritation at the dog.

"Mr. Nash asked me to come," said Edwina quickly. "Jillian Nash's father. He's out of the country, you see, but he's so sorry for your loss and he wanted me to ask if there was anything he could do for you or your family. But I'm afraid I must have gotten myself lost, somehow, and—"

She waved at the dirt road, the car, and the gate, making the gesture as woebegone and helpless as possible.

The girl's eyes narrowed further in recognition of Nash's name. "He's got a nerve. There's nothing he can do; what could there be? Come on, though, I guess you might as well go out the front way now that you've gotten this far. What did you do, try to get up here by following a map?"

Edwina reached through the Fiat's window to get it, first tossing the car phone's handset out of sight behind the seat.

"Yes. See here, Poole Road." She traced her route on the folded map with a finger. "Wasn't that right?"

The girl stepped nearer, peering over Edwina's shoulder. She smelled of toothpaste, soap, and shampoo, mingled with cold fresh air. "Oh, for heaven's sake, is that still on there? I'll have to get to get a sign put up before people start trying to bring dogs in here on that rut and get themselves stuck."

In the distance, Edwina could now hear a chorus of excited barks, yelps, and yips as if perhaps a hundred dogs had just caught sight of a hundred Milk-Bones. The Doberman pricked her ears at the sound, head tipped interestedly.

"That's right," Mrs. Bennington's niece told the dog, "now you're late for lunch. Serves you right for running off that way."

She opened the little white gate. "You must have gotten your directions from one of those old fools at the post office," she called back, and Edwina did not trouble to contradict this as she slid behind the Fiat's wheel.

"I swear they think they're still living in the nineteenth century down there," the girl said. "Well, come on, but drive slow. One of those mutts gets hit, I'm the one who's got to bury it." She shivered expressively, wincing. "And in this weather, pretty soon that'll take a jackhammer."

Edwina pulled the car through the gate, then stopped. The day was not very chilly, and nothing to what it would be like up here in another month: hip-deep drifts howling in on the storms called Alberta clippers, followed by day after bright still marrow-freezing day. But with her milk-white skin and flyaway blonde hair, probably this girl was the type to feel it more.

Edwina rolled down the Fiat's window. "I wonder if I could use your phone before I go? I'm running a little late, now."

Ahead lay the house, a two-story Georgian affair of white-painted brick with red brick chimneys and green shutters. Before it a wide, paved circle drive spread a formal welcome; behind it stood a number of long, low buildings like chicken coops, with rectangular yards surrounded by high lengths of chain-link fence. Inside the fences, dogs ran: dozens, perhaps hundreds of them.

Big dogs, little dogs; fat dogs, skinny dogs, some like the pictures in the purebred-breeder's brochures, others resembling little more than a geneticist's joke: stubby dachshund legs on beagle bodies, whippet tails on collies, pugs in spaniel coats. In one of the runs a fellow was filling huge troughs with kibble.

Mrs. Bennington's niece frowned, walking beside the car. "I suppose that's all right," she said. "I never did get to thank you for being so helpful the other night. The rest of them would have liked to write it off as some mistake, or something."

She stopped. Without being told, the Doberman paused at her heel and tipped its sleek head alertly.

"I'm Janet Bennington, by the way," the girl said. "Go on up to the house and park out front; someone will let you in. Or I hope somebody will, anyway. The whole place is going to hell without Aunt Berenice."

In the bright, nippy morning, the girl's face looked bluish and a bit desperate. The dog got up and tugged gently at the leash.

"You tell him, though," she said. "You tell Mr. Nash I said he's got one hell of a nerve."

* * *

"Hello?" Edwina called out, opening the big green front door and peering into the enormous entry hall. "Anybody here?"

Apparently no one was. Feeling fortunate that she had chosen to leave Maxie at her mother's—decidedly nonviolent, he was still capable of defending several hundred square yards of even the most difficult territory if only it happened also to have a dog in it—Edwina called once again, then stepped inside and closed the door behind her.

The house smelled of cinnamon, cloves, oranges, and dog. There was simply no disguising it: the smell of warm hound was everywhere, in the pre-Revolutionary knotty pine woodwork and in the Turkey carpets whose nap had been wearing thin before the first Independence Day.

On a small hall table beneath a maple-framed mirror, cards overflowed from a split-reed basket. Poking at these, Edwina peeked at their messages:

sympathies, condolences, and regrets. Most were from pet food distributors, animal husbandry suppliers, and purveyors of veterinary goods. A few were handwritten notes conveying formal but obviously sincere sorrow.

On a hook by the door hung a braided leather dog leash; in another basket beneath it were a grey knit cap, gloves, and a pair of ankle weights. Mrs. Bennington had been taking her exercise; at least the cap did not look like one Janet might wear.

Doctor's orders, Edwina thought, easing out the drawer of the little table and spying a prescription slip among the few old grocery lists, notes of library books to look for, and other bits of random domestic paper stuck there. The prescription was for nitro-glycerine tablets—two tablets as needed for chest pain—and it was dated a week before Mrs. Bennington's death.

Somewhere an old grandfather clock tick-tocked hollowly. Edwina slipped the drawer shut; as she did so, footsteps pattered from the rear of the house. "Hello?" she called again.

A tall, thin old woman in a lumpy cardigan and khaki slacks appeared at the back of the hall. On her feet were a pair of well-worn hiking boots, and in her arms she clutched a bundle of firewood.

"Excuse me," said Edwina, "Janet said it would be all right for me to use the telephone. Can I help you with that wood?"

"Not," replied the woman, "unless you've brought along some work clothes. Have you?" Amusedly she eyed Edwina's outfit of slim tan cords, Frye boots, silk blouse, and leather bomber jacket.

"No," Edwina smiled back, "I'm afraid I haven't."

"Step out of the way, then; there's chores to be

done and I guess I'll be doing them. You're not dropping off dogs, I hope."

"No, I just happened to—excuse me, but is this place a boarding kennel? Or do you raise dogs here?" The latter seemed unlikely; she could not imagine deliberately breeding the mixed bag of mongrels she had glimpsed outside.

She followed the woman into a sitting room where a black potbellied stove squatted, radiating heat. All around the room, on the knotty-pine walls and clustered together in shelves and on tables, were the ribbons, cups, and statuettes of dog-show prizes: best in show this, best of breed that, grand champion the other.

The woman released her armload of firewood into an orange crate, straightened, and dusted her hands together. "Not anymore," she said. "At one time, Poole Farm bred the best Gordon setters in the country, but that was back in the sixties when Mr. Bennington was alive. Now we're a dog dump."

"Grr," said a small, shaggy pillow tucked into an armchair; looking closer Edwina saw it was a Pekinese, or sort of one.

"We take charity dogs," the woman explained, "and keep them until we find homes for them. Shoo, Blinky, you know Janet won't like seeing you there. That's a people chair."

Yapping bitterly, Blinky scrambled from the room.

"You mean any dog?" Edwina asked. "They can just get left here, and no one ever—"

"Puts them to sleep? Heavens, no."

The woman brushed some dog hairs from the armchair. "That's the point of Poole Farm, letting them live. Poor Berenice, the lady whose farm it was, she passed on quite recently, she had a soft spot in her heart for unwanted animals. And Berenice could afford to do what she liked, you see."

"The soft spot," corrected Janet Bennington sharply from the doorway, "was in Aunt Berenice's head."

"Yes, dear," said the older woman, "we all know your views on that subject. But you and your friend had better run along; I've got my chores. Is Carl out feeding like I told him to?"

"He was," Janet replied. "Who knows what he's up to by this time? I don't see why you won't let me fire him, Zelda; he's the laziest man. And I *don't* like the way he looks at me."

The older woman pursed her lips deliberately, then thought better of whatever it was she had been about to say. Turning, she stuck out a sinewy hand and gripped Edwina's firmly.

"Bring your work clothes next time," she invited. "You look like a good strong girl, and we need all the help we can get. Don't we, Janet?" she added with a touch of asperity. Then she strode vigorously out, most likely to split another cord or so of firewood before lunch.

"Come on, Miss Crusoe," Janet Bennington said as a door at the back of the house slammed emphatically, "the phone's this way. Don't let Zelda scare you. She's been here so long, now, she thinks she owns the place."

"I thought she must be a relative." Edwina followed Janet to a bright country kitchen with an enormous brick fireplace.

"Sit," said Janet. "I started some coffee; I'm chilled to the bone. You might as well stay and have a cup if you want."

Edwina perched on a stool by the breakfast counter. Garlic braids and bunches of dried herbs hung all about; glass jars of beans, spaghetti, and rice stood on the scrubbed pine counters and violets bloomed on the windowsills. "I thought," she pressed casually again, "Zelda might be another of your aunts."

"Good heavens, no," Janet said, puttering efficiently at an electric stove where a kettle was already steaming, "she's an employee of Aunt Berenice, and before that of my uncle, I guess. She's an absolute workhorse, too, as I guess you saw, not to mention stubborn as hell." She poured steaming coffee into pottery mugs.

"Now," she said, sitting across from Edwina at the counter and wrapping her thin fingers around the warmth of her cup, "why don't you tell me what you're really doing here? Because I don't believe that line you pitched me in the yard for a minute, you know. You came to find out something, I'll bet, so why don't you just ask? It's a lot," she finished acutely, "simpler that way."

Edwina smiled in spite of herself. Janet Bennington was no fool and clearly no more afraid of hard work than Zelda, judging anyway by the tough crop of calluses on her blunt-nailed fingers.

Janet saw her looking; the tracery of tiny lines around her green eyes deepened. "Just a country girl at heart," she said thinly, "no point in manicures around here. You're trying to get her off, aren't you? The nurse, I mean; you want to show she didn't do it. You must be if you're hooked up with her father. Too bad I know she did, because I was there and I saw her."

Edwina's respect for this girl went up another notch. "You are very perceptive." She sipped her coffee, which was excellent.

"Let's just say I've had some good teachers. Zelda thinks I killed Aunt Berenice myself, I think." Her eyes hardened further. "Of course she'd never dare to say that, or even suggest it in her manners. She knows I'd toss her out of here in a minute if she did."

"You?" Edwina sized Janet up again: young, tough, and a lot more street-smart than any girl in her mid-twenties ever got on a rural dog farm. "But I thought—"

"Because I wanted her to agree with me about firing a lazy worker?" Janet shrugged. "I can't afford to antagonize her if I want to keep her. We live here together; it would be awful if we didn't get along. But Poole Farm belongs to me, now, or control of it does, anyway. The whole thing's in a trust, you see. Aunt Berenice set it up that way to keep her estate out of probate."

"Really. That was wise. And you're the sole trustee?"

The girl tossed her head of yellow fluff. "Wise? More like crucial. Can you imagine what inheritance taxes would come to on this place? You'd have to sell half of it for house lots, not that anyone would bother buying them. In case you didn't notice, poor old Deptford's not exactly a happening town."

She slid off her stool and carried her coffee to the kitchen window. Through it could be seen a wide, still-green lawn bounded on one side by a grape arbor, on the other by the pruned autumn skeletons of a dozen rose bushes, each bush neatly blanketed with root mulch. At the yard's end a small, open summerhouse looked over the valley to the foothills of the Berkshires and beyond.

"Which," said Janet Bennington, "is fine with me. I'm going to keep it all the way Aunt Berenice

118

wanted it: remote and quiet and perfect. Not that I've got much choice—the trust says I can live here and get an income, a salary for running the place. But I'm not allowed to sell it even if anyone wanted to buy, and I have to account for what I spend, quarterly, to the bank."

"Keep it the same," Edwina suggested, "except for the dogs?"

Janet's lips tightened. "Except for some of the dogs. This isn't an animal hospital. The place simply can't afford to be one without dipping into Aunt Berenice's capital. Zelda just doesn't understand what things cost, but dogs that come here really sick, they're going to have to be put down. Otherwise we'll spend more than the trust earns, and I refuse to do that."

She strode to the brushed-aluminum sink and set her cup down sharply in it. "Anyway, I'm afraid that's all I've got time for. I've got a hundred things to do today. Aunt Berenice's funeral is tomorrow, and there'll be people coming here afterwards."

Edwina got up. "I'm very sorry about your aunt."

"So am I," said Janet. "She was good to me. She didn't even know me a year ago when I showed up here broke and desperate. She didn't have to take me in, but she did, and she showed me how to live. Only . . . not how to live without her. She didn't get time for that."

The girl's lip trembled; she lifted her chin defiantly. "So does that about cover what you wanted to ask me, Miss Crusoe?"

"Yes," replied Edwina, opening her leather tote. "Yes, I think it does. And for what it's worth, I think your aunt taught you very well how to live without her, difficult as it must be. You seem to be handling everything capably. I'm sure she'd be proud."

119

She drew out a card. "Perhaps you'd take my number? In case there's anything I can ever help you with. You never know," she smiled as Janet hesitated, "it might come in handy."

A small frown creased Janet's forehead as she took the card, tucking it in her jeans pocket as she walked Edwina to the front door.

"Go out by the front drive; it takes you down to the county road," she said, scooping up a pile of mail from the little table in the hall. "Darn, Zelda's been to the mailbox already. I had some things to send. Now I'll have to go back out in the cold."

"I could take them," Edwina offered. "I'm going right by."

Janet looked doubtful at this but gave in as a chill breeze riffled the cards in the split-reed basket. "Just stick them in the box and put the flag up," the girl instructed as Edwina took the envelopes. "The mailman will stop for them on his way back to town. One advantage to living in the nineteenth century," she added with a little smile. "People around here haven't lost their old-fashioned work habits."

Then she caught sight of a young man across the front yard, languidly draping shrubs in burlap. At the rate he was going it would be a long time before he finished, which fact did not seem to disturb him. He paused to light a cigarette, saw Janet watching, and took a deliberate drag before flicking it away.

"Some people haven't, anyway," Janet said tightly, stepping back from the door and closing it.

As Edwina drove past him the young man dropped the burlap strip he was draping and stepped into the driveway, blocking it. "Nice car," he grinned, leaning with his big calloused hands on the door to peer into the window.

She waited while his gaze flicked over the Fiat,

then over herself. He was handsome in a spoiled, darkly boyish way, with thick, black lashes and a pouting lip above a deeply cleft chin. His sly grin offered an invitation so clear that it might as well have been engraved across his belt buckle.

"Guess she showed you the door pretty quick," he went on, as if hoping Edwina might join him in a session of Janet-bashing. But when she did not he tried another tack.

"Think you could maybe give me a quick lift into town? My car's acting up. And I need," he added, staring at the front of her shirt, "to pick up a few things."

"Sorry, I'm not going that way. You must be Carl."

He straightened with a pleased swagger. "She mentioned me, huh? Figured she would," he added with a low, suggestive laugh.

His tongue flicked over his lips. "Sure you don't want to give me a ride?"

"Sorry," she said again, dropping the Fiat into gear and pulling away. When she glanced in the rearview mirror, he was lighting another cigarette, staring sulkily after her as he cupped his fingers around the match flame.

But when she stopped at the foot of the drive he appeared again, striding down the hill toward her and grinning cockily. Quickly she stuck Janet's envelopes into the mailbox; as she did so she spied another envelope in the weeds, half-hidden by the mailbox post.

"Hey," he called, his bootheels clicking aggressively as he crossed the pavement. "Hey, don't go away mad."

She crouched for the envelope, saw the writing on

it. "I'm not going away mad," she said, straightening. "Just going away."

Swiftly he reached out and plucked the letter from her hand, his fingers brushing hers and lingering an instant too long.

"I'll give you a ride back up, though," she tried, holding out her hand for the envelope. "I guess Zelda must have dropped that. I'd better give it to her so you won't have to—"

"What?" he said, a challenge moving in his eyes; she should not, she realized, have made a point of it. "So I won't have to take time out from my menial chores?"

He grinned. "It's okay, I'll give it to her. Besides," he dusted his hands unnecessarily on his tight jeans, "I'm all grimy. Sure wouldn't want to dirty up the insides of that pretty car."

His look said that was precisely what he'd like to do. "I never should've asked," he drawled, "but now that you offer so nice, I'll take a raincheck for sometime when I'm cleaner."

"Fine," she said, sliding into the bucket seat and slamming the door. Fool, she told herself, dropping the Fiat in reverse, roaring backwards up the driveway, and turning pointedly out in the direction of Deptford instead of away from it as she'd told him she was going.

In the rearview mirror Carl stood grinning crudely after her, apparently immune to insult, one thumb hooked in his belt while the other hand absently fingered the envelope. If she hadn't let him know she wanted it, he would have given it to her; the writing on it couldn't possibly mean anything to him. He was just being provoking, goading her for turning down his come-on.

Blast, she thought, fingers tingling with the desire

to have that envelope again, to find out somehow what was in it.

Because while the handwriting could hardly be meaningful to Carl—it was doubtful, she thought, whether any sort of writing meant anything to that lout, except perhaps the kind inscribed on public restroom walls—it certainly was meaningful to Edwina.

It was the same writing as on the letters Barbara Moran had shown her the other night: the hateful and accusing letters Jill Nash had been receiving from Millie Clemens.

But why in the world would Janet Bennington be getting one?

* * *

Perhaps Wilbur Freeman was out scouting up customers for his séances. At any rate, he wasn't answering his telephone.

Mrs. Milton was, or rather someone was answering it for her; the widow of Jill Nash's supposed earliest victim had suffered a heart attack during the night, said the pleasant neighbor woman who picked up Edwina's call, and would not be seeing or speaking with anyone for at least a few days.

Standing at the pay phone outside the general store in Deptford, Edwina couldn't quite think of any way to ask this nice neighbor lady to sort through the sick widow's mail, pick out a certain envelope, open it, and read what was inside to a complete stranger—assuming Mrs. Milton had even gotten such an envelope, although Edwina was willing to bet she had. Writing to Jill's victims seemed just the sort of thing the angrily hysterical Mrs. Clemens might do, to stir things up and get some attention for herself, and if possible to make matters worse for Jill.

Dialling Mrs. Clemens's number, Edwina felt a moment of optimism as the receiver was picked up. But the moment she had identified herself and asked Mrs. Clemens what she wanted to know—people, in Edwina's experience, sometimes answered importunate inquiries before they had time to think, and with luck this might be one of those times—the receiver was slammed down again.

All right, she thought, striding musingly and stubbornly to the car; I have to see Wilbur Freeman anyway. Pulling the map from the glove compartment, she checked the distance: forty minutes, tops.

Maybe, she encouraged herself as the little Fiat's engine rumbled willingly to life, he'll be home by the time I get there. Maybe he'll even be brimming with useful information.

Maybe, she thought, not believing it for an instant.

* * *

Wilbur Freeman's house was a shabby old Victorian whose gingerbread trim was blackened and crumbling with neglect. Wet leaves spilled from the gutters, mildew stained the clapboards, and the porch sagged unsteadily before a row of tall parlor windows, their draperies tattered and their panes unwashed.

Making her way reluctantly up the weed-choked walk, Edwina felt the atmosphere of the house reaching out for her. Inside the smell of dust would hang like a shroud; a sour sponge would lurk on the kitchen drainboard and in the silverware drawer would be tarnished forks with dried egg clinging between the tines.

"Ain't home," quavered a cracked old voice from behind her as she steeled herself to knock.

Startled, she turned to the old man squinting unpleasantly from the yard next door. Bent almost double with age, wearing a red quilted jacket, plaid muffler, and galoshes, he leaned on a rake with which he had been scooting fallen leaves into a pile.

"Gone out, Wilbur has," the old man offered, twisting his neck to peer at her with suspicion. His face was shrivelled and brown as if carved long ago out of an apple.

"Been gone about an hour." He spat the words as if they tasted bad. "Mebbe an hour and a half. Went out right sharp after the mailman came by."

"Oh," said Edwina, watching as the old man speared a leaf and shook it grimly onto the little pile. Apparently he was of the rake-'em-as-they-fall school of autumn lawn maintenance, in sharp contrast to his neighbor; leaves in the Freeman yard lay in bright knee-deep drifts, probably with last year's leaf-fall soggy underneath them.

Uncertainly she crossed the Freeman porch, whose floorboards seemed dubious—if she were not careful her foot might go right through one of them—and cupped her eyes to try seeing through a parlor window.

"Gone, I say," insisted the old man, his metal rake making a monotonous musical sound as it scraped along his front sidewalk. "Old woman's gone, too. *She* won't be back a'tall. Croaked," he amplified with grim pleasure.

"Sorry to hear it," Edwina replied through gritted teeth, for there it was, inches away yet inaccessible as the dark side of the moon: another of the letters, open on the desk inside the window. All she could make out of it was "Dear Mr. Freeman."

"I don't suppose he said when he'd be back?"

The old man shook his head, not deigning to waste words on a woman who peeked through other people's windows. Stymied, Edwina descended the porch steps, not liking it that Wilbur had read a letter from Millie Clemens and immediately left the house. What could she have said to him?

This, she thought irritably, was turning into a wild goose chase, and there was only one help for it. She didn't want to ask Janet Bennington what was in her letter: for one reason, she would almost surely have to talk with Janet again, and the last thing she wanted was for Janet to begin thinking of her as a pest.

And for another, there might be something interesting or important in Mrs. Clemens's messages, in which case there was no sense Edwina's letting anyone else know that *she* knew it.

That left Mrs. Clemens herself, who if she knew the truth about Edwina's purposes would surely be even less eager to talk than she already was.

And *that* left just one choice available to Edwina: to look Mrs. Clemens in the face and lie.

"I'll tell 'im you was snooping," the old man yelled. His gnarled fist gripped the rake and shook it threateningly at her.

"Oh, good," she called back from the car, "do that. Tell him I want to buy his leaves, ten dollars a bag. Too bad," she added, "yours are all gone already. I'd have bought them, too."

A crafty grin split the old man's wrinkled-apple face; as she pulled away he was eyeing the Freeman yard covetously, rake twitching in his greedy fist. Now, you've done it she scolded herself; you're going to have to go back and buy those leaves.

But it was worth it to put one over on such a

grouch, and besides if he went on scraping at his own nearly leafless yard, the old man would rake himself to China. She made a mental note to herself, to ask Watkins to send a boy down with a truck, then spied a phone booth and stopped to call and ask at once, before the aged neighbor's industry could begin dislodging stones out of the Freeman house foundations.

"How's Maxie doing?" she inquired when Watkins had promised without hesitation to do as she requested; however many bushels of leaves Mr. Watkins got for his compost, he always wanted more and was glad not to have to rake them up himself.

"Tell you the truth," Watkins said, "'e looks a mite peaky. Nothing too bad, but—fella's had 'is shots and all, has 'e?"

A pinch of worry tweaked her. "Yes, he has. He's all up to date on everything. What's wrong, Watkins? Is he stomach-sick?"

"Nope. Just a little mopy. I'll keep an eye on 'im, Miss, don't you worry. Give 'im a drop of cod-liver if he don't perk up, shall I? You'll be here tonight, then?"

She frowned; heading back to Litchfield had not been in her plan. But— "I'll be there," she said firmly; poor Maxie.

"That's fine," replied Watkins, satisfied. "Nothing so good for the inside of an animal as the outside of its master, I always say. Or mistress," he added, "as the case may be. I'll tell 'im you're coming, most prob'ly that'll fix what ails 'im."

"Thanks, Mr. Watkins," Edwina said, hanging up reassured.

Minutes later she found the tiny frame house on a street of other frame houses just like it. Treeless, postage-stamp yards, concrete side driveways leading to one-car garages, short front walks to concrete-slab front steps whose ironwork railings bled rust-stains—the only thing different about the Clemens house was the aroma of boiling cabbage that hung about the door.

Which was not so unusual; horrid little houses seemed always to smell of boiled cabbage. Why, Edwina wondered, did a food that tasted so good have to smell so much like stewing socks?

She raised her finger to the doorbell and paused as another, unhappier thought struck her forcefully: *before*, Harriet had said, *someone else does*.

Because after all one would really have to boil quite a lot of cabbages before the smell could manage to seep outside the house, wouldn't one? And stewed socks weren't the only thing cabbages smelled like, were they?

"Mrs. Clemens?" Edwina hammered briefly, rattled the knob and found it locked. Scrambling down the front steps she dashed to the side door, which stood open a crack.

Through it poured a smothering reek, chokingly thick and unmistakable: cooking gas. Don't, she thought, touch a light switch, dial the phone, or even scrape a chair across the floor.

"Mrs. Clemens, are you in there?" Which was foolish; if she was, she was in no condition to say so. The gas-smell clapped itself to Edwina's face as she nudged the door wide, then spotted a woman sprawled across the kitchen table.

Gas hissed furiously from all four unlit stove burners. On the table by the woman's elbow were an empty teacup and a brown glass pharmacy bottle. Holding her breath, Edwina shut the gas off, thrust her arms beneath the woman's armpits, and hauled until the woman's limp body balanced upright for an instant.

In that instant she bent her knees, clasped the body lower, and shifted her weight—for if she had learned anything at all in her nursing years, it was how to make an unconscious person's body go where she wanted it to go—whereupon the body of Millie Clemens slid bonelessly off the chair, exerting its whole weight upon Edwina.

No patient of mine, she thought grimly, ever hits the floor; *no* patient. She staggered toward the kitchen door.

Ten steps, fifteen; Mrs. Clemens's fuzzy slippers caught on the threshold and slipped from her calloused heels, exposing a pair of bluish, arthritic feet.

Twenty steps; straining to stay upright, Edwina backed out the doorway and down the back stoop, past the milkbox and over a rubber door mat that read "Welcome."

Fifty steps; across the narrow driveway, past the trash cans, and into the neighbor's yard. Not, she thought, her breath now coming in ragged gulps, far enough.

"Call 911," she yelled to a woman peering wide-eyed out her kitchen window. "Ambulance and fire department—"

Dropping Mrs. Clemens's body on the grass at the far side of the yard, she flung it roughly over onto its back and probed at the throat for a pulse: nothing. Tipping the head back, Edwina blew two quick puffs of air down the body's windpipe and listened at its chest.

No breathing, no pulse; Edwina ripped the woman's housedress unceremoniously open. Kneeling, she laced her fingers one hand atop the other, pressing the heel of the lower one to the Clemens woman's flaccid chest.

One-one thousand, two-one thousand . . . cringing inwardly she felt the woman's rib crack, a grinding rice-crispies sensation accompanied by a faint, wet snap. Ignoring this—*later, I'll scream later*—Edwina sucked in a huge breath of fresh air and forced it into the woman's lungs.

This was not at all like CPR training. For one thing, the plastic dolls used for the resuscitation classes that all nurses took did not have blue, flabby lips; their chins were not slick with spit and their noses when you pinched them to force the air down into their lungs did not slip from between your desperate fingers.

And if you failed—or if the whole process was simply too repulsive for you—the practice dolls didn't die.

That, thought Edwina bleakly, bending to force another breath down Mrs. Clemens's windpipe, was the big difference. But as she thought this she heard a sound that flung her reflexively face-down across the woman's body: a telephone, ringing in the Clemens house.

Halfway through the first peal, a rumble shuddered through the earth. Edwina jumped up, dragged Millie Clemens's body one more hopeless step, and was abruptly knocked flat by the blast, the enormous broadside whack of it skidding her across the yard and slamming her headfirst into some box hedges, behind which fortunately someone had stored a discarded mattress and several surplus rolls of attic-insulating material.

By the time she got her wits back enough to know which end of herself was pointed up—rolling out of the hedges rather than into them posed, at first, a knotty intellectual challenge—fiery bits of Mrs. Clemens's kitchen roof were raining from the sky. The ambulance and fire trucks were arriving, too, although curiously without any accompanying sound.

On the grass a few feet away Mrs. Clemens's body lay like a tossed-aside rag doll, its arms and legs flung about randomly. Airway, breathing, pulse, Edwina thought, feeling her own limbs moving zombielike toward the victim.

Rough hands caught her from behind and turned her. A man's anxious, sooty face peered into her own. The man was wearing a yellow rubber suit, enormous rubber boots, and a yellow hard hat, and his lips kept moving exaggeratedly but soundlessly as embers and flaming debris continued falling.

"What?" Edwina yelled, but no sound came out.

The man in yellow seized her firmly, lugging her kicking and screaming—Or, she thought, I *would* be screaming if I could make any noise; why can't I make a *noise*?—to an ambulance where a young man dressed in paramedic whites urged her gently to a stretcher, then crouched reassuringly over her.

Or, she thought, it *would* be reassuring if only I knew what the hell was going *on* around here. . . .

Loudly—or it *would* be loudly—she demanded information.

In response the paramedic put a finger to his lips, pointing at her left arm to which he was applying considerable pressure with a fistful of gauze pads. Nevertheless the arm seemed to have a surprising lot of bright red blood streaming down it; also there was a long, thin dagger of aluminum siding about the size of a railroad spike sticking out of it.

Urgently, Edwina made writing motions with her other hand; the young man reached back, snagged her a tablet on a clipboard, and thrust his ballpoint pen at her.

"I can't talk," she printed roughly, balancing the clipboard on her knees which had really begun trembling quite a lot, now; all that adrenaline, she realized, racing around with nowhere to go and nothing superhuman to do. Her head was beginning to feel a bit swimmy, too. Very swimmy, in fact.

The young man read her message, made a face, and scribbled back one of his own. "You can talk," he wrote. "You just can't hear. *Big* boom." He waved an arm to indicate the size of the explosion.

"Oh, is that all?" Edwina said silently, passing out.

SEVEN

"I'M not doing this on purpose, you know," Edwina told William Bell as he frowned crossly over her in the emergency room of Chelsea Memorial Hospital. "I mean, I didn't go out and get injured just to give you more work to do, I hope you realize."

Bell grunted in reply. His face was haggard, his eyes puffed and reddened, his clenched jaw shadowed with a day's worth of unshaven stubble. Forgotten in his shirt pocket by his pen was a Hershey bar he had not gotten a chance even to unwrap, much less to eat; watching him scribble her admitting assessment on a chart, it occurred to her that he probably needed an intravenous more than she did.

Much more, actually, although just at the moment she did not feel up to convincing anyone of that. Besides, she was already getting one. Frowning, she regarded the clear plastic bag of glucose and saline hanging above her and to her left, connected by clear plastic tubing to the IV needle in her hand. To her right, wedged in against the stretcher railing, were her clothes, purse, and shoes, all stuffed into a brown paper shopping bag.

Also crouched to her right was a scrub-suited surgeon, now busily engaged in stitching up her arm with a suture needle curved like a fishhook, after having removed the aluminum dagger lodged—rather firmly, as she had wincingly discovered—in the tender flesh and muscle there.

"Sure you're okay with this?" he muttered, not looking up.

His voice came fuzzily through a hiss of annoying static; her ears, while already beginning to recover, still felt plugged with cotton wads. The effect was of having one's brain hooked up to a pair of defective loudspeakers wrapped in blankets.

"Little deep, here," he went on, "and this needle's kind of big. I can numb it up some more for you if you want."

Edwina blinked, as in her experience a surgeon's ability to notice pain varied inversely with the amount of pain being felt, assuming of course that the surgeon was not the one feeling it.

"That's okay," she assured him, marveling at the wonderfully anesthetic effects of a little unasked-for sympathy.

"Actually as long as I can hear myself scream," she went on, "I don't care if you use a rivet gun. You have no idea how relieved I am not to be stone deaf—the arm is the least of it, to my mind."

He nodded. "Yeah, well, I'm glad you can take it so calmly. While you're at it, though, try being relieved to be alive. If that hunk of shrapnel had zigged instead of zagged, it could've ripped open your aorta instead of this little chunk of muscle mass I'm sewing up here. What the hell were you doing, anyway?"

"I was trying to give CPR to a lady who—oh. Will, what happened to her? Did Mrs. Clemens come in here? Is she—"

Jerking his head toward the next curtained cubicle, Bell looked sour. "Right next door," he gestured tiredly. "And my congratulations on the save, by the way—another critical ICU patient; just what I needed. I'll be up until four with this one, easy."

Then he stopped, rubbing his forehead exhaustedly. "Hell, I'm sorry, Edwina. It was a great save, honestly. Christ, I'm so wiped out, I hardly even know what I'm saying."

Which just at the moment hardly mattered, for Edwina was no longer listening to him. Nor was she listening to the surgeon, who as he finished tying off the final suture was lecturing her on the importance of at least twenty-four hours of IV antibiotics and preferably forty-eight, to prevent a nasty deep-wound infection from the dirty chunk of foreign object he had so skillfully extracted.

Instead, she concentrated on a querying voice from beyond the curtain, in the next cubicle where Mrs. Clemens lay.

"Why?" the voice said. "Why would she do it that way?"

The surgeon stripped off his gloves. "All finished. Just hang around a day or so, suck up some bug-killer." He gestured at her IV. "Deep sutures dissolve; you can take the superficial ones out yourself in a couple of days. You know the drill, right?"

"Right," she frowned, still straining to catch the next-door voice. But it was impossible; trying to hear two things at once made them both dissolve into a muddle of static.

"Can't I do the antibiotics myself?" she asked the surgeon, "at home? After all, I'm a nurse. If I can take out my own stitches, what's the big deal about sticking a few doses in an IV bag? I've done it a thousand times for other people."

"Well," the surgeon replied doubtfully, "I guess you could. Thing is, the best drug for this situation's kind of toxic. It's new, not approved for use anywhere but in-house. 'Course," he nodded toward Bell, "if your main doc here fills out a bunch of forms and you sign a release, pharmacy will make an exception . . ."

William Bell's shoulders sagged. Behind him, a man stepped from Mrs. Clemens's cubicle: wrinkled and baggy-eyed, pudgy and balding, wearing a brown tweed suit and an aging, striped silk tie.

His authoritative bearing identified him as a physician; no other visitor kept even a shred of bearing in an emergency room, where the air seemed to carry some confidence-corroding substance that ate like acid into even the most assertive personalities.

"Will," Edwina said, "ask that man if I can talk to him a minute."

Bell looked mutinous. "Listen, Edwina, right now you're just an ordinary minor trauma case, and I've got to get you squared away so I can see my other patients. I haven't got—"

Sadly, the old physician turned toward the door of the ER's trauma-admitting ward.

"Will," Edwina said evenly, "you get him over here before he leaves and I won't make you fill out all those pharmacy forms. Otherwise I'm getting out of here right now, even if you have to do paperwork until *your* arm needs surgery. Got it?"

The surgeon glanced from Edwina's face to Bell's. "You know," he began, "I think she's offering you a pretty good—"

"Done," snapped William Bell. "Sir?" he said.

"Excuse me, sir, but this lady over here would like to—"

Slowly, the elderly physician turned from the doorway, his eyes scanning the cubicles professionally. In his face Edwina saw brains and discipline, mingled with the kind of unfooled resignation that came from half a century of taking care of sick people.

"What is it, Doctor?" he said, emphasizing this final word; the ghost of a sympathetic memory curved his lips as he took in Bell's age, situation, and general level of misery.

"This nurse, here, Miss Crusoe—she did the resuscitation on your patient Mrs. Clemens," Will told him, "and she'd like to have a few words with you."

The old physician brushed past Bell and elbowed the surgeon aside as he made his way swiftly to Edwina's stretcher and seized her hand.

"You," he said. "Thank you, my dear. I'm Dr. Greenspan, and I do appreciate your good work very much."

His faded blue eyes radiated a youthful light, tempered now by the knowledge of a probable coming grief. It struck Edwina, though, that he was something more than Mrs. Clemens's doctor. Or perhaps he only wished to be, for surely no ordinary physician held back so many tears with such determined dignity.

"You think she tried suicide," said Edwina, not bothering to soften the words; this doctor was clearly too old and experienced to tolerate that. He would want the straight story; the rest, said that penetrating gaze, was merely bedside manner: a pleasant fringe benefit when patients wanted it and one could summon it, perfectly legitimate at most times and never precisely a lie.

And worthless when push came to shove. As it was right now, Edwina thought through the hum in her ears.

Her mention of suicide seemed to trigger his wish to confide in someone. "I gave her," he said, "enough chloral hydrate to fell a horse. She was in my office just yesterday; I wrote her another prescription for it. But only because she seemed to be doing so well. She was sharp, she was better—she was almost happy," he insisted, shaking his balding head.

"But maybe I was wrong," he went on, his voice heavy with regret. "Maybe Millie was fooling me."

He looked up, his eyes requesting a truthful answer. "So tell me," he said, "was I wrong? Did I help my old girl try to kill herself? Did she," he pressed, "smell of chloral?"

Edwina met his gaze. Behind him, the emergency room's usual routine—order barely imposed upon chaos—continued: scuttling lab techs, striding physicians, racing nurses, and harassed clerks making their hurried way among the constant streams of walking, rolling, or unconscious wounded. Over it all hung the smells of rubbing alcohol and Lysol-soaked floor mops.

"No," she said, "there was no odor of chloral on her breath. I very much doubt she'd taken any—not recently, at any rate."

Greenspan's face relaxed, then pinched in perplexity. "But," he repeated, "why, then? Why that way, when she had—"

Bell cleared his throat impatiently. "Edwina, we really do need to finish getting you into—"

"Yes, I know," she snapped at him, having had quite enough of other people's urgent reasons why she ought to do as they wished, at once and without argument. "Finish admitting me to a hospital where I don't want to go and don't need to be, so that somebody else can give antibiotics I'm perfectly capable of administering to myself. All right, let's get on with it. But Dr. Greenspan, you come visit me, will you please? And—"

She beckoned him nearer, to whisper to him. His immaculate neck smelled of laundry starch and lime shaving cream.

"Bring Mr. Clemens's medical chart along," she told him, "the notes of his final admission. You can get them, can't you?"

Straightening, Greenspan patted her hand avuncularly, his eyes searching hers. "Of course, my dear, I'll be happy to do that. I'll see you later, then."

But in his glance as he turned to stride dapperly out, she glimpsed the beginnings of comprehension, as her request had shed swift new light upon his question: why would Millie Clemens try suicide by turning on all the gas jets when she had a much better, simpler method at hand? And even if for some reason she wanted to take gas, why not take the chloral, too, just to make sure?

A more pertinent question, of course, was why she would try it at all.

Calmly Edwina lay back once more upon the stretcher and let the patient-transport technician take her upstairs. Greenspan had made the connection at once, which meant Mrs. Clemens had told him of her suspicions: that her husband had been murdered.

Which—no matter how many autopsy reports might say his death was a natural one—Edwina now thought he almost certainly had been, and Greenspan was realizing it, too.

Probably, Edwina thought, Mrs. Clemens had said it to a lot of people. The trouble was, none of them had listened, so she kept on saying it. Finally, or so Edwina was willing to bet, she had written it: first to Jill Nash, then to the survivors of the other victims.

And to one of them her letter had been an unwelcome surprise, provoking a swift, sure, and murderous reaction.

Only, she thought with grim satisfaction, shifting obediently from stretcher to hospital bed, not quite sure enough.

It was in this triumphant mood that she telephoned McIntyre, once she had gotten settled and been left blessedly alone. After reassuring him—yes, she was a patient in the hospital; no, it wasn't serious, and no, he needn't dash up to sit by her bedside, it was just a little cut, really—the fact that it had taken twenty-two stitches to close was something she figured he could just as well find out later—Edwina got down to the real business of her call, which was that as far as she could tell, Jill Nash was off the hook.

"Because look, Martin, it's obvious someone tried to kill Mrs. Clemens because of her letters. Otherwise it's simply too big a coincidence, you see. Someone wanted to stop her telling something she said or hinted at in what she wrote. And if that someone wasn't Jill, which if she's got an alibi for early this afternoon it couldn't possibly have been—"

McIntyre listened silently, which was odd in itself and would ordinarily have alerted her.

"—*which* she surely must," Edwina went on. "All she does is lie at home and Barbara Moran is there until two o'clock or so. And *that* means someone *else* wanted to shut Mrs. Clemens up, someone who's the *real* guilty one in all this—"

McIntyre continued silent. "Doesn't it? Martin, will you say something?"

For a moment she feared her hearing might have gone out on her again, but when he did speak she almost wished it had.

"Jill was supposed to be at a hearing downtown this morning at ten o'clock," he told her quietly. "When she didn't show up, her lawyer called her house. That was around ten-thirty. Jill wasn't there, so he talked to the Moran woman. Jill's bail was revoked and an arrest warrant for failure to appear was issued on her about twenty minutes later, on the basis of what Moran said."

"Which was?"

"Jill was ready to go at around nine," McIntyre recited. "At nine-fifteen she went out to pick up a couple of things at the nearby drugstore, got back about ten minutes later. Moran heard her open the mailbox out front, expected to hear her come in. When she didn't, she looked out and found Jill gone, along with Moran's car, and nobody's seen or heard a thing from her since."

Blast and damn. "So she's got no alibi. On the contrary, in fact."

"Right," confirmed McIntyre.

"And we don't know she *didn't* get a Clemens letter this morning," she went on.

"Right again, but it looks like something she got in that mail made her run, something she hadn't planned on. Moran says right up until the minute Jill disappeared, she was flat-out set on the hearing. No hesitation, no maybe-I-won't-show-up stuff. She meant to be there."

"Drat. Now I've got to call her father, tell him she's gone and if she doesn't show up he forfeits a quarter-million. He's going to just love that one. *And* he's going to blame me."

McIntyre made sympathetic noises; they helped, but not much, because on top of everything else the Novocain she'd gotten in the ER was beginning to wear off. As a result her arm felt as if that surgeon really had used a rivet gun, and as if he were in fact still using it now: *thump, thump, thump,* dull bolts of pain in time with her pulse.

"I tell you, Martin," she said, "I'm about to give up on these people. Nash's an utter twit, Jill's a dim-witted brat, and I'm sick of both of them. And my arm hurts, too," she concluded glumly. "I wasn't going to tell you that, but—oh, *drat* that stupid girl, anyway. Whether or not she's guilty, why does she have to behave so much as if she is?"

"Maybe," suggested McIntyre, "*because* she is?"

"Maybe," Edwina conceded. "I just wish the whole thing weren't so darned neat, that's all. Even really guilty people don't look as guilty as she does—unstable background, unsavory motive, a history of being accused of the same thing earlier, as if she came in a kit labelled Contents, Good Suspect. It bothers me, Martin, and something else is wrong about it, too."

"Oh? Such as?"

"Such as," she said, "what's the silliest idea for a B-movie hospital murder story you can think of? The oldest chestnut in the world? A doctor or a nurse running around sticking poison in people's IV tubings, that's what. Leaving aside that once in a while it does happen, I still don't—it's just that the more I think about it, the more it feels to me like someone made it up."

She heard her own voice growing more complaining. "Anyway, I think I'll take a walk, get my mind off my miseries. I've got one more thing to check"—Walt Clemens's chart notes, which had looked potentially revealing a little while ago but now seemed utterly unpromising —"and if I don't get anywhere with it, I guess I'll have to call Ted Nash," she finished discouragedly, "tell him I've just plain struck out."

"Hmm, I suppose. No rush, though, is there?" he suggested tactfully. "You could wait until you feel better."

She laughed in spite of herself. "You mean I sound so awful I shouldn't inflict myself on him?"

"You sound," he replied, "wonderful, and you are wonderful. I haven't told you that often enough lately. Nor," he added, "that I miss you—this bachelorhood business is a bore."

The thump of pain in her arm eased at the words; she leaned back against the bed gratefully.

"But just give it twenty-four more hours, why don't you?" he added. "I say that as a cop who's had his tail saved more than once by just sitting tight, waiting for things to develop."

She sat up at once. "You know something," she accused, "you found out something new, and you're not telling me—"

"Nothing," he replied soothingly, "that you don't know yourself. I've been listening to you, that's all. You're very enlightening sometimes, Edwina, did you know that?"

"*Martin*—"

"Nurses," he chuckled, "running around putting poison in the IVs. It really is a silly idea, and familiar, too. So familiar, it just might work."

Still chuckling, Martin McIntyre hung up.

Monster, she fumed silently at him as she got out of bed and into her clothes. Whatever his idea was, he wasn't going to tell her—not, at least, until he had checked it out himself. She would simply have to wait for his report.

With care she was able to get her IV-arm into her shirtsleeve. The jolt of pain that assailed her as she did so was more than made up for by escaping the hospital gown, since while she might have to act like a sick person she most certainly had no intention of confining herself to the costume.

Besides, sitting tight and waiting for things to develop was against her nature, and going against her own nature always made her irritable. I will walk, she told herself firmly, and think. But as she gave the rolling IV-pole an impatient shove toward the door of the tiny private room, a wing-tip shoe appeared on the linoleum before it.

"I've got Walt Clemens's charts," said Hiram Greenspan, his round, brown-suited body bulking in the doorway. One plump hand gripped the handles of an old leather doctor's bag, the other clutched a manila file folder. "And you," he went on, "aren't going anywhere until you look at them with me."

Edwina stared. It had been not more than half an hour since she'd asked for these charts. In order for him to be here with them now, he'd had to go straight to the medical records room, make his request, deal with all the excuses and objections the secretary would offer against his ever getting what he wanted, much less getting it immediately, and then bully, bribe, or otherwise railroad a medical-records clerk into fetching it for him this instant—since deceased patients' charts were warehoused in the hospital's basement, never—usually—to be seen again.

But this apparently was what he had done. "Dr. Greenspan," she said, stepping back to let him into the room, "you are my kind of guy."

Greenspan eyed her in bulldog fashion as he tossed the folders on her bed. "I as much as told Millie she was nuts," he said. "Now she's upstairs on a respirator. I'm wondering if I should've listened harder, if maybe this whole thing's my fault."

"Oh, really, I don't think you need go so far as—"

"Besides which," he said, "you come around asking questions. You're that snooping nurse, been written up a couple of times in the newspapers, aren't you?"

Edwina admitted to being this nurse. "I was on my way to ask Mrs. Clemens a few things," she said, "when—"

"Hmph. Guess I'd better be thankful for that. Looks like you did a damn fine job, too," he added gruffly. "They told me in the ER her pupils were reacting—she's got brain function on account of you actually got her ventilating and circulating, not just going through the motions like some of them idiots do."

"Oh," said Edwina softly, swallowing the sudden lump of emotion in her throat. That, she realized, was the other thing about resuscitating a real person as opposed to a rubber doll: when you failed, the rubber dolls didn't die, but when you succeeded, they didn't live. Only people did.

"Anyway," he went on a bit more gently, "it doesn't take a genius to put it all together. You think maybe someone did kill Walt, or why would you want to see his records? Millie was sure someone

145

did, and she said so loud and clear. Which I'll bet was her mistake, saying it once too often."

He eyed her shrewdly. "That about your diagnosis?"

"You know, Dr. Greenspan," Edwina replied, "you're so smart, you've almost made my arm stop hurting just by being here."

He dropped into the chair beside Edwina's bed. "No, I'm not smart, and I hope to hell I remember it from now on. I'm an old fool who should've put an arm around Millie, believed her when when she told me she had pain, and when she told me plain out, too, where it was coming from."

He looked grimly angry at himself. "Instead, I prescribed her a drug. And that's what's wrong with modern doctors, among whom I blush to admit I must now include myself. We think we're so damned smart, so much smarter than those foolish old women who clutter up our offices and take up our time with their complaints. Poor Millie. I love her, you know. If she dies, I'll never forgive myself."

His eye fell on the charts. "On the other hand," he said, "I didn't turn on those gas jets, did I? And I'll bet neither did she. She isn't stupid. And I don't see how anyone could've slid a murder past an autopsy, but—"

"Let's have a whack at trying to see how," Edwina said, picking up the folders in which the last few hours of Walter Clemens's life were recorded. "Who knows, maybe we'll get lucky."

Even as she said this, she did not particularly believe they really would. The chart, after all, had been gone through at the time of the postmortem exam, and in addition was not likely to be in very good order, since no one had planned ever to have to consult it again. But half an hour later they did get lucky, because the chart was in even poorer order than she expected.

Which was how murder had indeed been slid past an autopsy, and why the sliding of it had been simple.

*   *   *

"Potassium," said Edwina, staring at the chart pages spread before her. "So harmless, so commonplace."

She looked up at Greenspan, who glowered at his clenched fists. Suspicion was one thing, but now he knew Clemens had been murdered. "Harmless," he growled, "unless you get a big dose all at once."

He slammed a fist into the palm of his hand. "Then, boom," he said. "And that cuts it, doesn't it? Millie was right, that nurse shot Walt full of potassium."

"I'm not so sure," Edwina replied. "It would have been easy for her to do, that much I agree with. But she would have known—look. He came in and had his gallbladder removed, routine surgery, and everything should have been fine. But then—"

She flipped through the chart pages. "Two days later he starts having blood-pressure swings, and they put him on drugs to keep his pressure down. Only the drugs work a little too well, he loses his pressure entirely, gets brought back with fluids and more drugs—this time, naturally, pressure-elevating drugs."

All of which, although unfortunate, was not so unusual; blood-pressure drugs took some tuning to get the dosage right. One or two episodes of hypotension were undesirable but par for the course, and didn't turn into disaster for most patients. They had, however, for Walt Clemens.

"Walt," said Greenspan disgustedly, "was just too decrepit to get well after losing his blood pressure twice."

"Right," she agreed. "He went over like a row of dominoes, and as near as I can tell his next problem was kidney failure."

"If he hadn't drunk so much beer all his life, maybe—"

"His kidneys," she continued, lining up the events in her mind, "were borderline to start with, and big-time hypotension delivered the final blow. So after *that*," she turned a page, "they put him on dialysis, to clean the substances out of his blood that his kidneys couldn't take care of. And one of those substances happens to be potassium."

She frowned at the chart pages. "Three times a week kidney dialysis: Monday, Wednesday, and Friday. He died Friday night. Serum potassium levels during his final resuscitation were seven, and postmortem they were nine. Not high enough to kill a well person."

"But enough," Greenspan said, "to mess up his heart muscle, put him into fibrillation. Resuscitating him from that knocked a clot out of his heart, where probably it had been sitting for years. Bingo."

So Walter Clemens's hospital course had been downhill from the word go. And the autopsy pathologist hadn't noticed anything unusual about the high potassium level, because—

She rummaged at the back of the chart, where a clutter of lab slips and other bits of paper were stuck: paperwork that had not yet been filed when Clemens died, but had eventually caught up with the folder and been inserted in it.

Meanwhile, no pathologist would ignore an elevated potassium unless there were some reason to.

"Here." She held up a list of chemistry lab results, and the kidney-dialysis procedure note to which it had been stapled. The note was a description of routine kidney dialysis, done four hours before Walt Clemens died. The lab slip with it showed his postdialysis potassium level as 4.5, which was as good as normal.

And that was the missing information. Without a procedure note, the autopsy pathologists had no way to know that day's dialysis had been done, and thus no way of knowing that the high potassium level drawn during the resuscitation was remarkable. They simply attributed it to kidney failure in a patient due for dialysis, instead of an oddly high reading in a patient who'd just had the potassium-lowering procedure performed.

Nor had they any way of knowing the level had been 4.5 just four hours earlier. If they had, they'd have realized at once: nothing but a big, unscheduled dose could make a serum-potassium level go up so much, so fast.

Only, the lab slip and dialysis note had been delayed, first in the dialysis department, then in interdepartmental mail, and finally in medical records. Since no one realized it existed, no one had searched for it. The chart went from the ward to medical records, from there to the state medical examiner's office, back to Chelsea's records room, and finally into storage.

At last the papers had made their way into the chart, but not until after the patient's death was chalked up as a natural one.

"But," said Greenspan, "the nurse was the only one who—"

"Hiram," she interrupted him patiently. "If you know the drug is detectable, and I know the drug is detectable, don't you think Jill Nash must know it, too? No one could plan a records foul-up like this one, and anyone with access to the drug knows as well as we do that it shows on serum analysis. Whoever gave that stuff expected it was going to show up at the autopsy, and either didn't care or wanted it to be detected."

She folded the chart sheets back into their manila folder. "In fact," she added thoughtfully, "no one could plan a series of events like the ones that killed Walt Clemens, either. If he hadn't already had a clot waiting to break loose, the potassium by itself might not even have killed him."

"I don't see," objected Greenspan, "what any of that has to do with Millie, though."

"As a matter of fact," she went on, feeling as if she were tugging on a slim thread that might come loose or break at any moment, "the whole thing seems sort of slapdash. Like a kid with a chemistry set pouring random things together, just to see what will happen."

She looked up. "What if it was an experiment, just to try something out—of *course*. To try out the *method*. Because all along, Hiram, what's been stumping me is how anyone *but* a nurse could have done it. Someone with access to the patients *and* the drugs."

He nodded slowly. "And you think whatever the method was, Millie saw it happen?"

"Uh-huh. And *thought* she saw Jill Nash do it."

Enlightenment dawned in his eyes. "But," he said, pressing plump fingertips together, "what she really saw—"

"Indeed. She really saw someone else giving Walt

potassium in some way we have not managed to figure out, and something she wrote in one of those letters told someone else she did."

He nodded more vigorously. "And the letters—"

"Either say or hint what the method of administration was. We can probably get hold of one of them. *And* no one else knows we know about them, which gives us a bit of a—"

The phone on the bedside table rang. "Yes," she fumbled the receiver up impatiently, "what is it?"

But when she heard the message Martin McIntyre had asked to have relayed to her, all her irritation vanished. "Wonderful," she said, added a bit of information to be sent back to McIntyre, and hung up well-pleased.

"Jill Nash," she told Greenspan, "is in custody, charged with the attempted murder of Mrs. Clemens. She'll also likely be charged with Mr. Clemens's death, as soon as Lieutenant McIntyre gets my message. You say Millie Clemens is still upstairs on a respirator. Will she be on it overnight, did they tell you?"

He nodded, frowning. "She's still unconscious. But what's so wonderful about—"

"Good, then Patient Information will be giving her condition out as critical. Perhaps by tomorrow we can even think of a way to have her declared dead."

Greenspan looked outraged. "Now, listen here, Miss Crusoe, you've seemed like a sensible enough young woman so far, but—"

"Oh, not legitimately dead. Just . . . convincingly. In case anyone calls in to ask about her, because it does strike me her death will make someone feel even more secure, don't you agree?"

His face smoothed as he understood. "Secure enough to make a more few mistakes. Yes, I see."

He got up, gathering his bag and the folders. "Thank you again, Miss Crusoe. I appreciate your giving an outdated old coot like me a chance to help."

She smiled through a wave of pain; now that her mind was not occupied, her arm was beginning to throb insistently again.

"Don't thank me yet. We know there's a method, or we think we do. But we still need to find out what it is."

His glance went communicatively to her intravenous tubing.

"Especially," she agreed, "as I am now susceptible to it."

She'd meant the remark as a bit of black humor, but half an hour later the black part was rapidly increasing while the humor part decreased.

An anxious call from Barbara Moran conveyed the news that Jill denied having gotten any letter, from Millie Clemens or from anyone else. And whether or not this denial happened to be true, for the present it blocked the simplest way of finding out what Millie wrote.

Thus Edwina was forced to go to plan B, one involving much painful and so far fruitless operation of the telephone. The Bennington number was busy; the Milton number went unanswered. Wilbur Freeman's rang a dozen times but was at last picked up. But Wilbur did not want to talk about letters; he wanted to talk about money, which it seemed he was in even more imminent danger than before of being fresh out of.

After making her way through five minutes of his flowery outdated speechifying, she managed to make clear her reason for calling him, and then to conceal her wish to throttle him.

"Wilbur, what do you mean, you've burnt it? How could you possibly do such a . . . yes, I *know* you're stupefied with grief, but . . ."

Privately, Edwina decided Wilbur Freeman was stupefied not so much by grief but by the conditions of normal living—specifically, by the need to earn his. Now that his mother was dead, some small trust fund apparently was being terminated; most of his distress as far as she could tell came from finding himself even more penniless than he'd thought.

His story, meanwhile, was that he'd read the letter, flung it down in a fury at what he termed an impertinent intrusion on his private misery, and gone out to walk off his anguish. Upon returning he'd touched a match to the horrid missive, determining neither to acknowledge it nor to think of it again. Nor could he remember precisely what was in it, only that it was some sort of crude attempt to play upon his deepest and most sensitive—

"Thanks, Wilbur," she cut him off unfeelingly, hanging up.

Just as unfeelingly, she dumped him in her mental "suspect" bin; anyone who got a Clemens letter but who was unable to produce it, she decided, would henceforth be suspected of hiding it no matter what the excuse. And after all, Wilbur was cash-hungry; despite his delicate sensibilities he might have been expecting the trust fund to turn out rather differently. . . .

Musing over this, she dialled Mrs. Milton again; knowing the lady herself was indisposed, she still thought she might inveigle some helper or visitor into reading the letter aloud—in, she decided, whatever smoothly deceitful and utterly dishonorable way turned out to be necessary.

Her honesty and honor, although not her temper,

were saved by the fact that once again no one answered the Milton telephone. But when she retried the Bennington number, it was picked up.

"Poole Farm," said a crisp voice she identified as Janet's. Swiftly Edwina outlined what she wanted, although not precisely why she wanted it.

"Oh, yes," Janet said at once. "Awful thing, the poor woman seems to think she's tied up in all this somehow, although why she would want to be I can't imagine. I suppose all sorts of people think they're involved in things that get into the papers. But you want me to read the letter to you, is that it?"

"If," said Edwina, "you wouldn't mind."

Whereupon Janet did: "'Dear Janet Bennington,'" she read, "'I am a grieving person just like you, my husband was murdered by that nurse, too. And I saw the whole thing only nobody would believe me, so I didn't know what to do. But now the truth is out, I am so sorry for your loss. I saw just how she did it, it is in my mind like a photograph of her working that dial on the tube to make the poison go in faster. I wish you would call me, it might be I can tell you something else to help you. Sincerely, Mrs. Millicent Clemens.'"

"Isn't that," said Janet when she had finished, "just about the saddest thing you ever heard? Especially since it can't be true. I called Aunt Berenice's doctor and he said this Clemens woman is . . . well, kind of loony on the subject."

"Yes," Edwina said mildly, "it is sad. But rather odd, too, don't you think? She doesn't say she saw Jill Nash put any substance into the IV, only that she saw her make it run faster."

"Oh," said Janet. "That's right. Well, maybe she doesn't understand what she saw. But I know what

I saw," she finished firmly, "and it wasn't just turning up Aunt Berenice's IV tube."

"You saw Jill Nash enter the room, put some medication in your aunt's IV, then drop one vial in the wastebasket and another in her pocket. Is that it, exactly?"

"I saw her drop one vial in the wastebasket, and something else in her pocket. I didn't see that it was another vial until afterwards. But otherwise that's exactly right."

"And she didn't do anything else while she was in the room," said Edwina as a new thought occurred to her. "She didn't first mix something, for instance? Draw liquid from one vial, inject it in another, then put the resulting mixture into the intravenous?"

"No," said Janet positively, beginning to sound a bit more impatient. "And if you don't mind, I'm really very—"

"Yes," said Edwina, "you're busy. Thanks, Janet, I appreciate this." More, she thought as she hung up, than you realize.

For if Janet were telling the truth, Jill had prepared Mrs. Bennington's medicines as usual at the medication cart, in full view of anyone who might happen by or need to get something from the cart—hardly an opportune place for medicine tampering.

Of course, she might have done the actual tampering earlier, in the relative privacy of the nurses' locker room or even at home, before beginning her shift. But that still left the questions of why any tampering had been necessary, and why Jill had gone to the trouble of incriminating herself so thoroughly.

Why not simply draw up a syringeful of pancuronium, dispose of the pancuronium vial, and inject the IV directly? The vial could be left at home or in the trash, the tainted syringe dropped into the sharps-disposal box, which was at least a less suggestive place for it than one's own pocket. Instead, the pancuronium had been substituted for the Inderal, while the emptied pancuronium vial had not been gotten rid of at all.

On top of that was the doubt over whether the pancuronium had killed Mrs. Bennington. If it had not, what had it been for? And how could anyone but Jill have done all that was necessary, not only to get the pancuronium vial into her pocket, but to get at all the other victimized patients—all her *own* patients?

But it was the tainted Inderal vial that bothered Edwina most, at the moment. There was simply no good reason for it. Something was definitely missing, here.

"Hello, Miss Crusoe," said the pretty young nurse who came in just then, "I've got your medicine here for you."

"Fine," said Edwina absently, and then it hit her. "Wait a minute, let me see that, please."

The nurse was in her early twenties, small and slender with curly black hair, brown eyes, and a bright, reassuring smile. Without demur she handed the tiny bottle of antibiotic to Edwina.

The manufacturer's label read "Greosulfazine, 1000 units USP." Below that in tiny letters were the maker's name, an expiration date, and the words "dilute with sterile water immediately before administering—do not store solution."

"A lot of patients are looking over their medicines pretty carefully, lately," the young nurse said, "after all the uproar we've been having around here. Are you satisfied with that?"

"Yes," said Edwina slowly, "I am. What do you do with this vial, once it's emptied?"

The nurse took the vial back and tore off the metal tab-top, exposing the rubber stopper beneath; then with a small syringe she drew the fluid from it.

"I put it in your medication drawer," she said, "so when the drawer goes back down to the pharmacy for refilling they'll know to charge you for the dose. That's the way it works for all the drugs pharmacy can't mix up in advance."

She squirted the drug through a rubber port into a clear cylindrical chamber below the IV bag, then turned a little dial to fill the chamber with fluid from the IV bag itself.

"Although," she added, "to tell the truth it usually sits in my pocket, first. I sort them all out and put them back in the patient's med drawers at end-of-shift. It's simpler to do it all at once while I'm charting."

She jotted a brief note on Edwina's clipboard. "That way," she explained, "I know the vials in my pocket are from doses I gave, and the ones already in the drawer were given on the shift before me."

Which made perfect sense to Edwina. "But if pharmacy had sent up the dose already mixed, so you didn't need to save the vial for charge purposes, then what would you do with it?"

The nurse turned off the IV fluid's flow and dialled up the flow rate on the tube leading from the cylindrical chamber. By doing so she could rapidly administer the drug mixture, then switch easily back to the standard lower flow of undosed fluid from the IV bag itself.

As she watched the fluid-drops merging to a stream, it struck Edwina that if by some chance the vial hadn't held greosulfazine she might begin feeling some unwanted side effects rather soon. Probably it had, of course; still she was delighted not to note her vision blurring, her digestion cramping, or her consciousness waning, all of which she would have regarded as bad signs.

"Then," said the nurse, inspecting Edwina's IV site for any redness, swelling, or leakage, "I'd toss it in the wastebasket. No point in keeping it, and my pockets are full enough already." With this and a last professional glance at the IV's flow, she strode cheerily out.

It occurred to Edwina to call Janet Bennington back. But no; there was a simpler way to learn what she needed to find out.

Simpler . . . and perhaps more reliable. It was now nearly five o'clock, but Anne Crain didn't keep banker's hours. Dialling the pathology department, Edwina found her there, sounding harried but cooperative as usual.

"Oh, Lord," she said when Edwina had asked the question, "yes, the Bennington chart is still right here on the pile. The medical records runner was supposed to pick it up today, but—"

The sound of pages turning came through the phone. "History and physical, progress notes, temps and blood pressures . . . here we are, the pharmacy order sheets. You want to know what, now?"

"What drugs she had ordered for every four hours. So she'd get them at noon, four, eight—"

"—midnight, four A.M. and eight A.M.," Anne finished for her. "Let's see, she had Valium Q6, nitropaste Q6, Feosol Q6 . . . here it is. Two Q4 things, Inderal and penicillin. Inderal for her heart, and penicillin—well, actually a penicillin variety, neoxycillin—"

"Terrific. Neoxycillin's new, right? I've never given it. Do you happen to know how it comes? I mean, is it a liquid or a powder, a suspension—"

"Got my handy *Physician's Desk Reference* here," Anne said. "Let's have a look."

More pages turned. "Indications, precautions, warnings, side effects," Anne recited. "Ah, here we go. It's a powder. A pale-blue, crystalline substance. You shake it up in sterile saline before you give it— not to be stored in solution, sayeth ye olde *Physician's Desk Reference*, or drug decomposition leading to severe tissue necrosis may occur. Is that what you wanted?"

So there had been a third vial. Edwina sank back onto her bed. Her arm now felt four times bigger than the rest of her body, not to mention eight times meaner.

"That," she told Anne, "was just what I wanted to know."

Hanging up, she forced herself to her feet. An experiment, she thought as she pushed the IV pole toward the door, but not exactly an experiment. Really, the whole thing now seemed more to resemble . . . a riddle?

Yes, she decided as she made her way down the corridor, passing the medication cart with its little plastic drawers full of mixed and labelled drugs, passing the nursing station where the nurses' staffing and assignment lists were clearly posted, and heading out of the patient ward toward the service elevators.

A riddle indeed, simple, daring, and immensely wicked: when is a murder method not one?

The answer, she thought as she waited for the elevator to arrive—unlike the public elevators, this one would take her to the hospital's basement where the pharmacy was located—was that Mrs. Bennington's pancuronium had not been used to commit a murder, but rather to conceal one.

And this idea she could check with little trouble, or so it seemed until the elevator reached the basement and the doors slid silently open again.

EIGHT

HIS name tag read "Carl Wagner, Pharm. Dept." and his dark-blue cotton jacket told Edwina he was some kind of messenger—of course, she realized, a pharmacy runner—but the lazy grin and slicked-back dark hair were the same as she'd seen at the Benningtons'. Carl the dog-farm helper was also Carl the hospital pharmacy technician.

And that, of course, was the final connection, the one she had come down here to make: you didn't need to get directly at patients themselves, if someone else could, and *you* could get at their medicines.

Get at them, and switch them. Which meant the culprit might in fact be somebody from pharmacy—only not alone, and not a pharmacist.

As if to prove the correctness of this idea, Carl leaned casually against the tall, many-drawered pharmacy cart. Probably he was about to head out on a delivery run, but first he was absorbing the attentions of several young female nurse's aides.

". . . meet you at dinner break," he drawled. "You can catch me up on all the gossip I've been missing. I just don't know what I'd do without you ladies to keep me well-informed."

A chorus of giggles rewarded this witticism, as with relief Edwina watched the elevator doors begin closing. He hadn't seen her yet, and with any luck he wouldn't.

But at the last possible moment a hand plunged through the narrowing gap to stop the doors; in response the elevator bounced back open automatically.

A ward secretary stepped in, clutching some lab slips. "Sorry," she said, pressing the "up" button. Then, unaware of the disaster she'd wrought, she gazed boredly at the elevator-inspection card framed above the buttons.

The thump of the bouncing doors made Carl Wagner glance up; eyes narrowing, he recognized Edwina and his face flattened, his superficial good looks draining away to reveal his true personality.

Then the lazy smile returned; the elevator closed on it. He doesn't care, Edwina thought, but how could that be?

When the doors opened again, though, she understood: he hadn't been about to make a delivery run at all. Instead he had been returning from one, and now the "Code Five" emergency call began sounding on the overhead paging system, summoning members of the resuscitation team to the intensive-care unit where Millie Clemens had been admitted.

"Excuse me," said Edwina, pushing her way out on the lobby floor as a half-dozen visitors crowded into the elevator, "I do really have to—excuse me."

"Some *people*," spluttered an enormous lady in an enormous fur coat, and of course Edwina refrained from explaining precisely where the lady could put her coat, her opinions, and her elbow, which had narrowly missed Edwina's ribs.

Gasping, she dragged the IV pole behind her and staggered to a house telephone, which luckily no visitor happened to be using to make any of the long, pointless, argumentative phone calls all hospital visitors seemed to feel were their god-given right, not to mention their moral obligation.

"Let me talk to William Bell," she said when the secretary in the intensive unit had at last answered.

"He's busy right now," said the unit secretary, trying to sound professional and failing utterly as her chewing-gum popped juicily. "Can I take a—"

"You tell Dr. Bell he's got a patient dying up there and unless he talks to me right now she's going to keep dying, have you got that? Now go tell him this instant, young woman, and spit that cud out of your mouth. You sound like Elsie the Cow."

"Well," breathed the secretary, outraged, but a moment later William Bell came on.

"Don't talk," she snapped at him, "listen. Whatever's going on with Mrs. Clemens, it's coming from an unordered drug, either something she's allergic to or an overdose, probably an overdose of opiates. Try reversing it with Narcan, and if that doesn't work treat her for anaphylaxis. Got that? Don't thank me, just do it—and I'll talk to you later."

Assuming I *can* talk, she thought, hanging up just as the door to the service stairwell opened and Carl's face appeared, a furious mask beneath the glowing red Exit sign. He had something in his hand, something he palmed tightly against his narrow hip.

Whatever it was, Edwina didn't think she liked it.

Another bunch of visitors arrived at the elevators. Moving among them, Edwina made her way toward another door and another corridor, this one leading to the emergency wing and the clinic admitting areas.

Here feverish children wailed as harried parents bounced or cradled them; prep-school sports stars lounged uncomfortably with their coaches looking on anxious-eyed, nursing injured elbows or extending swollen knees. Bruises, contusions, abrasions, stomach pains, headaches, hemorrhoids, gout, gallbladder—all, after normal doctoring hours, came here to the city's biggest and best-equipped emergency room.

And a lot of them came by taxicab. Which meant there were often empty taxicabs *leaving*—

"Miss? Oh, *miss*," called an alert emergency room triage nurse, "do you have your doctor's permission to—"

Edwina swung around to confront this irritatingly correct person, coming face-to-face with an old, extremely battle-scarred colleague: white hair, wrinkled black face, crisp-pressed white uniform and sharp, unflappable expression.

"Edwina, what in the world are you—are you all right?" The old nurse assessed Edwina's wounded arm and IV at a glance. "What in heaven's name are you—"

"I will be all right," Edwina bit the words out swiftly, "if you tell anyone who asks for me that I went that-a-way."

She pointed back toward the lobby area. "Please, Jeannie."

The tough old nurse nodded shrewdly. "Go on then, get out of here. I don't know what you're up to, but it looks like more fun than what I'm doing."

She waved at the congregation of sick people over which she presided eight hours an evening and five evenings a week, every other weekend and holiday included. Then she grinned, pressing Edwina's hand briefly in her own. "Go on," she repeated, "I'll tell 'em you went that-a-way, whoever they are."

Edwina went. Outside the ER's sliding doors, the evening air was thick with exhaust fumes: ambulances, taxis, private cars. From one of the taxis just now gliding up to the sliding doors, an enormously pregnant woman swathed in mismatched thrift-shop clothing was exiting laboriously.

Glancing back, not seeing Carl, Edwina slid past the woman into the cab, hauling the IV pole behind her. The driver looked relieved to be getting rid of the pregnant woman, who was clearly about to deliver any moment, and only slightly doubtful at the IV equipment; the cab, fortunately, was a roomy old Checker.

"No drinkin', no smokin', no radios, no drugs," he recited in a pleasantly musical Spanish accent, tiredly levering the car into drive. "Where you wanna go?"

The Fiat was still parked outside what was left of Millie Clemens's house. Edwina gave the address and sank back against the cab's upholstery, which smelled sweetly of Armor-All. As the cab pulled out she noted the St. Christopher medal on the dash, the paper towels and glass cleaner stored on the window ledge, and the floor mats, which looked to have been scrubbed with a toothbrush.

The driver himself was small and slender with a neat, dark mustache, glossy black hair styled in a ducktail, and muscles that strained the sleeves of his immaculate white T-shirt. The small gold stud in his earlobe and the blurry letters tattooed on his knuckles said he'd gotten those muscles in a prison gym, probably.

"Listen, I'm very sorry but I'm rather short of cash—"

Before she could finish he had braked sharply to the curb, pulling up hard beneath a streetlight. "Come on, lady, I gotta living to earn out here, why you wanna pick on me?"

Trying not to dislodge her IV needle, Edwina dug painfully in her pants pocket. The cabbie turned, still grousing, stopped when he saw her come up with the ring she'd taken off in the ER so the IV could be taped in. The sight made him unhappier.

"Lady," he said in exasperation, "this item here iss worth a lot more'n one ride, you don' wanna be flashing a thin' like—"

On the cab's dashboard beside the St. Christopher medal was a studio photograph of a dark-haired young woman holding a baby.

"So you know the real thing when you see it, do you?" She turned it so the stones shone fiery in the streetlight's glow.

"Course I do," he began impatiently, "but—"

She nodded at the photograph and medal, her gesture widening to take in the cab's perfect cleanliness, his obvious pride in his own independent little business—and his reluctance to look too long at the ring, lest perhaps it prove a temptation to him.

"So do I," she said. "Hold this for me until tomorrow; I'll find you and pay you then, double the meter and more."

The cabbie sighed, pulling back out on the street. "Tha'ss my trouble, you know? I'm too sof'hearted, even my PO says so. Tha'ss my parole officer. You wanna trus' me with a thin', it makes me wanna trus' you, too, and tha'ss how I get in trouble."

He glanced in the rearview mirror. "You sure you wan' a excon holding for you? Iss okay, I'll take you

166

anyway. We're halfway there." He sighed. "Wha' the heck, I'll pick up a fare over on Whalley Abenue, prob'ly."

His hack ID said his name was Luis Ramirez. "What were you in jail for, Luis?"

He chuckled ruefully. "Cars. Any kin' you want, I get for you. If it got wheels, I can steal it, deliver to your door." He glanced at the dashboard photograph. "Tha'ss all done now, though. All finished history."

He swung the cab over. "Okay, here we are. You call up the dispatcher tomorrow, he tell you where I—whassa matter now?"

Edwina stared out the cab window. There at the curb where she had left it sat the little Fiat Spyder with its apricot paint job, black canvas top, custom wheels, and Pinin Farina body.

"Tha'ss a nice little car," said Luis softly, gazing at it. "Real pretty, an' it looks like you keep it real nice, too."

"Yeah," said Edwina disgustedly, "too bad it won't start. I left the keys with my money, back in my hospital room. Blast."

Then she looked up at the cabbie speculatively. "Luis, did you just tell me you could steal *any* kind of car?"

His neat small-boned face clouded with dismay. "Oh, no. I tole you tha'ss all finish now, otherwise they send me back to—"

Five minutes later he had the Fiat's door open, the hood popped, and the engine running. "You *sure* this is your car," he implored her from behind the wheel, "you *guarantee* me on your mother's *blood* this is—"

"Luis, the glove compartment is open. Inside is a tire gauge, a road map, and a blue envelope with my

167

insurance card, my registration, and a little leather bag with some quarters in it. There's a cat harness under the right-hand seat, a black umbrella on the floor behind it."

Luis sighed, sliding out. "Okay, it's yours, I guess. But I don' think I'm even gonna tell my PO about this. Maybe I'll jus' give you back your ring, too, an'—hey, what're you doing now?"

His eyes widened as she peeled off the adhesive tape, easing the IV needle from the back of her hand and dropping it. "Can't very well get all this in the car with me, can I? Don't worry, I can have it put back in later. But you've got to keep that ring, Luis, because I want you to do one more important thing for me."

Luis's eyebrows knit suspiciously. "Wha'ss that?"

She settled in the seat, flexing her good hand and wishing she were not going to have to shift with the other one. But there was no help for it. "I want you to call up a man named Martin McIntyre and tell him where I went. He's got to believe you right away, see, and if you've got that ring, he will."

The cabbie looked mutinous. "You gotta phone in there," he pointed out, "how come you don' jus' call him up yourself?"

"Because I'm too crippled up to use it while I drive," she answered, "and besides, I need it for something else. Which now that you mention it, I'd better start, it might already be—"

She picked the handset up clumsily, tapped in the Bennington number and heard Janet answer, then broke the connection and at once pressed the "re-dial" button.

"Please, Luis—" The Bennington phone rang again. "—it's important, and I'm going to make this worth your while, I swear."

Janet answered; Edwina waited, hung up, and redialled.

No reply from Luis but a stony glance; in response to it she summoned every bit of the persuasiveness she could muster even as she pressed "redial" again.

"Listen, Luis, wouldn't you rather have a job inside, in the hospital? I can arrange that. Regular hours, sick pay, vacation time—it's a good deal, Luis, and lots safer than driving cab, your wife would like that part."

Heck, she thought, if they could hire Carl they could hire this guy; she was well-enough known around Chelsea Memorial that she could swing it, and if not, maybe Watkins needed somebody.

Janet Bennington answered the phone again. "Listen, whoever this is," her voice came tinnily from the handset, "you'd better stop calling here. I'm taking the phone off the hook now, so you just stop." Exasperated, she slammed the receiver down.

Excellent, thought Edwina, hoping Carl hadn't yet thought of the telephone himself. Later he would, of course—just to make sure she pressed "redial" a final time and heard a busy signal—but by then he wouldn't be able to get through.

"Come on, Luis, I've got to go. Are you going to help me?"

Luis shrugged reluctantly. "Well, okay, I guess. But it's still gonna cost you," he warned, "I gotta living to make here. I ain't out here for no private amusement value an' my kid don' eat promises, neither. But anyway," he ended in grudging tones of surrender, "who's this McIntyre guy you want me to talk to?"

She dropped the Fiat into first gear, heard the satisfying grumble of the carburetors. The arm was bad, but not so bad she couldn't use it, and she thought she could keep pressing "redial" often enough to keep the Benningtons' phone busy, too. Later she planned to scream in agony for a year or so, but—

"He's a cop," she answered, fumbling the seatbelt down and managing to snap it, gritting her teeth against the bone-jarring misery this action produced. "A homicide detective."

"Oh, *madre Dios*," Luis Ramirez moaned sadly, "I thin' maybe I shoulda jus' kept the pregnant lady."

* * *

Twenty minutes later she had left the city behind; the cold, abandoned smokestacks of the factory towns stood bluely against a darkening sky. Leaving them behind, the concrete ribbon of Route 8 began curving and climbing into the first gentle foothills of the Berkshires.

Zooming down the next-to-last exit before the throughway came to an end entirely, Edwina made her way by memory through a maze of left and right turns, down a series of tree-lined narrow country lanes, and finally to the town of Deptford.

The little general store was still open, yellow light from its windows falling on the gas pumps and the bed of gravel where two cars and a pickup truck were parked. Edwina left the Fiat idling and bought a box of Milk-Bone biscuits and a smaller carton of dog treats from the teenage boy behind the counter, paying him with the toll-booth change from the glove compartment. When she went out again it was fully dark, and the Benningtons' telephone was still busy.

An enormous blue-white moon shone through the skeletons of the trees, brightening the unpaved track leading off the blacktop and up toward the rear of the Bennington place. Edwina doused the car's lights and crept along, hoping the sound of the engine would get lost in the bramble thickets. Her bad arm felt huge and clublike, every movement a bone-deep excruciating thud, but there was no bleeding, the dressing was still snug and dry, and her other hand was fine if a bit superficially tender.

She coasted to a halt and shut down the Fiat's ignition before the tires hit the pea gravel, and walked the last quarter-mile to the low, white gate, carrying the boxes of dog treats. Not every animal on Poole Farm was likely to be as friendly as Ruby the happy Doberman; unfortunately, she could think of no handy bribes to pacify the human animals inhabiting the place, and these were the ones she was most worried about.

Thinking these things, Edwina hurried across the side yard, feeling naked in the bright white moonlight. No movement showed at any of the windows in the big house, and no cars were parked in view; apparently the last of Mrs. Bennington's mourners had departed.

Surprise, she thought, scanning the windows at the rear of the place: I do break and enter, or at least I do when I'm provoked enough. And while Ted Nash's money was insufficient provocation, Carl's recent try at blowing her to bits was plenty.

Of course, he hadn't known she would be in Millie Clemens's house. But he'd known Millie would be, since he was the one who had left her in a kitchen full of cooking gas and set the chloral bottle beside her to make it look like suicide, probably after he bonked her on the head to make sure she would stay there a while. Long enough, for instance, so he would have time to drive to a pay phone and dial Mrs. Clemens's number, and trigger the boom.

Edwina ducked among some box hedges just as the first dogs caught scent of her; a series of high, excited yelps floated from the kennels, joined almost at once by the others: growls, yaps, howls, and a low, full-throated baying that sounded unpleasantly like a bloodhound. Head down, she scuttled along the hedgerow and had nearly reached the back porch when the yard lights went on and the back door swung open.

"What's the matter with them?" came Janet's irritated voice from somewhere within the house.

Zelda stepped out, peering across the yard. In her right hand she held something darkly glinting. A pistol—startled, Edwina was surprised at herself for not expecting it. Two women, mostly alone way out here. And Carl was as likely to be trouble himself as any stranger.

At least to one of the women in this house he was. But to which one?

As if in answer Zelda moved across the porch, hefting the pistol expertly. "Raccoon or something out by the runs," she called back to Janet. "Maybe a skunk." She strode across the yard, intent on the grimly pleasant chore of varmint extermination.

Swiftly scanning what she could see of the kitchen and the hall beyond, Edwina slipped onto the porch and through the open back door. Knowing what Carl had done was one thing; knowing how and why—and proving it—was another.

And unless it had already been disposed of, the proof was in this house. Holding her breath, she flattened her back against a wall as Janet passed by the kitchen door, then passed it again with a large buffet tray. On the tray were some stacked coffee cups and scattered remains of little sandwiches; she was, Edwina saw, cleaning up after the reception visitors.

Which meant she would soon find Edwina in the kitchen—the sharp, smacking report of a twenty-two pistol echoed from the darkness beyond the yard lights—unless of course Zelda got back here first.

Rule number one for housebreakers: if you must get caught, let it be by the person who does not have the gun. The idea propelled Edwina down the little hall, around the newel post, and halfway up the big front staircase before her foot hit a creaky tread and Janet's voice stopped her.

"Zelda?" Janet's shadow fell across the hallway.

No, Edwina thought irritably, crouched out of breath in the darkness of the upper stairwell, it's Carmen Miranda. The box of Milk-Bones was sliding from under her arm, but she didn't dare shift to get a grip on it; any instant the biscuits would rattle downstairs and scatter on the floor at Janet's feet.

Blessedly, Janet's shadow went away. Edwina let her breath out, prayed the staircase had just one creaky tread, and reached the first-floor landing without raising further alarm.

To her right were a bathroom and a small sewing room with an old treadle Singer raised up on an oak case. Beside it Edwina could make out a dress dummy with pieces of light-colored garment draped on it. A housedress, it looked like.

The sight cheered Edwina: the dress appeared too large for Janet, and Zelda did not seem at all the housedress-wearing type. That meant more of Berenice's things might still be here, too; letters, papers, possibly even the contents of her purse.

Surely no one here wanted to commit the offense

of dumping the dead woman's belongings, as if to say that one was glad to be rid of her; not, at least, until after the funeral. Better by far, certainly, to keep all in innocent-looking normalcy, just in case someone did come around with questions. For in that case it would be easier to pretend one did not understand the significance of a thing than to explain why one could not produce it, in the event it should be asked for.

All of which encouraged Edwina as she paused in the darkened doorway of the first bedroom, and sniffed. Cigarettes and scented face cream: Janet's room. Edwina shone the flashlight just long enough to glimpse the books heaped messily on Janet's bedside table: thrillers. Snapping the light off, Edwina moved on to the next door.

Here the faintly rank odor of lanolin mingled with the doggy smell Edwina had noticed earlier. From it she concluded Zelda had her own pet, some canine who at least at nighttime enjoyed upstairs privileges—only please not that horrid little yap-dog, and especially please not now.

But as no yaps came from the darkened room, she moved on to the third doorway. From it floated a rich, nostalgia-producing fragrance: lavender-scented bed linens and Estée Lauder dusting powder.

Closing the door of this room behind her, she checked that the window shade was lowered, set down the box of Milk-Bones, and switched on the flashlight. Berenice Bennington's bedroom held a single bed covered in blue polished chintz, a dressing table skirted in the same material, a chest of drawers, and a bedside table with a reading lamp. Her closet was organized with military neatness, as were her dresser drawers: swiftly Edwina lifted sweaters, underthings, and stockings, probing among them fruitlessly.

The whole plan must have revolved around getting Mrs. Bennington to the hospital, where her death could be hidden among the murders of other patients. Therefore, there was some way to get her there, and Carl's presence in the pharmacy suggested what that way had been. But—

Three pocketbooks nestled together in another of the dresser drawers: one each for spring, summer, and winter. Each, however, was stuffed with nothing but tissue paper, and the autumn purse—the one Berenice had been using at her death—was not there.

Drat. Edwina turned to the bedside table, slid its drawer open without optimism, and stopped. Inside lay a worn, leather-bound prayerbook, a packet of tissues, a tube of hand cream, and a small, orange, plastic pill bottle that rattled when she picked it up.

Hardly daring to hope, Edwina shook a tablet out onto her palm, then plucked it up and pressed it against the skin under her tongue. The warm, faintly tingly sensation it made said it was nitroglycerine, Berenice's legitimate heart medicine.

Disappointed, she spat it out. Substituting fake nitro could have made Berenice's chest pain seem to be getting worse and sent her into the hospital, but this bottle at any rate held the real thing.

A sound from the hall made her hurry to replace the small container, which slipped from her clumsy hand as she bumped it against the bedside table. Tiny pills scattered on the floor.

Cursing inwardly she crouched to retrieve the dratted things, forcing her fingers to move despite the pain this caused. Ten, a dozen . . . one by one she plucked them up, dropped them into the bottle, then examined the floor under the bed for any she had missed and spotted one.

Frowning, she aimed the flashlight's beam onto the tiny tablet. It was smaller than the others. Not enough to notice unless one had the other tablets right there for comparison, but . . . tasting the final pill, she winced at its piercing sweetness.

Saccharin. This tablet must have fallen at some other time and lain there unnoticed, the bottle refilled with real medicine later. But how could she not have tasted the difference at once, if indeed she had been taking saccharin?

Anne Crain's words came back: ". . . old stroke . . . anosmia . . . loss of taste and smell." According to the chart it hadn't been considered a major problem.

Slowly, Edwina shook her head. Maybe Mrs. Bennington's doctors hadn't thought it any major problem, but odds were good that Mrs. Bennington had. She'd recovered very well from her stroke, with one important exception: she could have poured a salt-shaker into her mouth and tasted nothing but sand.

The thought filled Edwina with sadness at what the old woman's life must have been like, as one by one its pleasures vanished until experience consisted mainly of medical routines: pills and potions, tests and procedures, the impersonal confinement of the doctor's office and the hospital room.

But one thing she could still sense clearly was pain—pain that did not ease, because she took saccharin, not heart pills, and couldn't taste the difference. Pain that sent her to the hospital where Carl Wagner had murdered her.

Carl . . . and someone else. Grimly Edwina pocketed the small, damp tablet, slid the bedside table drawer closed. As she did so she heard once more a sound behind her, still faint but now much too near for comfort.

My ears, she realized, but it was too late now to curse her diminished hearing, for at this point the sound was not only audible, it was recognizable: a dog.

A large, growling, extremely suspicious dog; slowly, Edwina turned. Nudging open the bedroom door, Ruby the previously happy Doberman paused, hackles raised and lips curled snarlingly. It seemed meeting strangers outside the house was one thing, inside quite another—or so the creature's stiff-legged gait suggested as it advanced.

"Ruby," tried Edwina softly, "good dog, want a treat, girl?" With extreme caution, she reached behind her for the Milk-Bone box lying on the bed.

A low, angry growl froze her arm halfway back. The only snack this animal wanted was fresh meat. Too bad, she thought with a giggle she knew was rising panic, I'm attached to mine—

The dog sprang. Rolling back onto the bed Edwina kneed upward, struggling to fling the furious creature off. Hot animal breath gusted in her face as the dog barked wildly, jaws clicking and slavering as it pinned her.

"Ruby," she gasped, "damn it, you're supposed to be man's best *friend*—"

Shoving, she scrambled from beneath the beast, grabbed a bed pillow and shielded her face with it. The dog slid away on the bedcover, scrabbled back at once, and renewed its attack.

Last chance; Edwina aimed a kick at the dog's ribs, putting all her desperation behind it. *Sorry, dog*—

"Ruby, down!" The snapped command came as the bedroom light glared on; as if also controlled by the switch the dog jerked its sleek head around alertly, leapt down from the bed, and trotted to stand by its mistress, panting.

Checking herself for bites Edwina found only claw marks, no punctures, which was fortunate as it didn't look as if she would be receiving any tetanus boosters or rabies vaccines anytime in the near future. On the contrary, in fact.

"Good dog," murmured Zelda, reaching down to pat the animal but keeping her gaze—and her gun— aimed steadily at Edwina.

"Well-trained," Edwina managed, wondering if her plan might have worked if she'd brought along a few fresh sirloins; the only Milk-Bone that could possibly have satisfied Ruby was the kind made exclusively for attack dogs, flavored with human blood.

"Very well-trained," replied Zelda calmly, "as you've just discovered. Now I think you'd better come downstairs and explain exactly what you're doing here. If," she added, "you can."

Shakily, Edwina followed Zelda from the room, thinking fast and coming up with absolutely nothing. Being caught snooping around inside the house pretty much ruled out any of the innocent explanations she might devise, at least on such short notice.

Which left telling the truth, or some of it. Janet came into the hall with a dishtowel in her hands as they reached the bottom of the staircase. "What was Ruby—oh."

The girl's brow furrowed, her glance going at once to the phone on a table in the parlor. It was still off the hook, although Edwina thought that was not going to help her much, now.

"I'm calling the police," Janet said, striding to the phone and seizing it.

"Wait." Zelda motioned Edwina ahead of her, into the room where the woodstove's fire glowed warmly behind an isinglass screen. "I want to hear this. Go on, sit. And remember, Ruby is very obedient."

Under the dog's watchful eye, Edwina obeyed. Curtains drawn and lamps glowing, the room with its heavy pine furnishings and colonial knick-knacks—pewter mugs and plates on the sideboard, antique embroidered samplers framed on the knotty-pine walls—was a perfect illustration of old New England coziness. Only its air of determined secrecy lent a false note, as palpable in the air as the faint scent of wood smoke, but nowhere near as sweet.

"Why," demanded Zelda, "were you in Berenice's room?"

Face flattened to a look Edwina could not fathom, Janet sank into a chair. "What," she breathed, "is going on here?"

"That's what I came to find out," Edwina said, "although I think I already know quite a lot of it. From the start, you see, I couldn't quite believe Jillian Nash had murdered your aunt."

"But I told you, I *saw* her—"

"I know what you told me you saw—a nurse injecting your aunt with a fatal drug. And what struck me even at first was how old-hat that idea was, so late-night-movie perfect. And everyone saw the vial come out of her pocket. How utterly convenient, and the fact she was so suspectable worked well also."

Janet shook her head, looking dismayed.

"Especially," Edwina added, "as she'd had a similar incident happen two weeks earlier. Real-life crimes aren't often so neat."

Zelda's face darkened. "What are you talking about?"

"I'm talking," Edwina replied, "about your handyman, whose evening job you neglected to mention happens to be at Chelsea Memorial Hospital, in the pharmacy department."

She glanced from Zelda's face to Janet's but neither woman reacted. "The plan," she went on, "really worked very well—as it ought to have, considering the planning that went into it. Months, I'd say, to get everything set up."

She turned back to Zelda. "Finding a victim was the most difficult chore—a victim, I mean, who would be blamed for Mrs. Bennington's murder. Carl had to hear a lot of gossip, I'll bet, before he found Jill Nash. Hospital gossip, in which her name kept coming up. Her money troubles, her personal life—"

"This is ridiculous," said Janet, reaching once more for the phone. "You're simply making up a lot of—"

"Shut up, Janet." Zelda's hand with the gun in it looked steady and capable. "Go on, Miss Crusoe."

Tight-lipped, Janet worked the dishtowel between her nervous fingers. "I don't see why we have to listen to this."

"Berenice was going to sell Poole Farm, wasn't she?" Edwina guessed. It was, at this point, the only possible explanation. "Sell it and divide the money between you—half for Zelda, the faithful old family retainer, and half for Janet, who's only been here a year."

She turned to Zelda. "You didn't think that was fair, did you? After all, why should you lose your home, the only way of life you'd ever known, just so this little upstart could get hold of half the estate?

180

The money itself meant nothing to you—it's Poole Farm you care about, the house, the land and animals, your history here—no amount of money could replace that."

"Liar," breathed Janet, "you vicious— How can you even say such things when we've just finished burying her? Zelda loved Aunt Berenice as much as I did; she never would hurt her."

"The trust arrangement must have been a blow," Edwina said, not taking her eyes off the weapon in Zelda's hand. "Berenice gave Janet complete control of the place, stipulating only that she couldn't sell it. Insulting to Zelda, who'd been here for so very long, but Janet was blood kin and that was that."

Zelda's chin came up. "I told her whatever she wanted to do would be fine with me."

"I'm sure you did," Edwina replied, "until she changed her mind. She must have seen how unhappy Janet was here. Lots of hard work, long cold winters, few young people about—except for Carl, of course, and she wouldn't have thought he counted. Not really much of a life for a pretty young woman, Berenice must have decided. And when she had decided something, she couldn't be talked out of it. Am I right about that much, Janet?"

The girl now eyed Zelda doubtfully. "She did what she put her mind to, Aunt Berenice. She could be . . . bossy. I heard them arguing, sometimes; I knew she was thinking about selling. But she wanted to sell the place whole and there weren't any buyers."

"Not yet." The curtains were not drawn quite shut. A small crack showed headlights swinging around and winking out.

Let it be McIntyre, Edwina thought, dry-mouthed; let him be here now, before I run out of story.

"But," she said, "there would be a buyer some-day. It could happen any time. Meanwhile, despite her ailments Berenice really was quite a vigorous old woman, and under constant medical care too, so her good health was well-known. For her to die suddenly at home would have looked too suspicious for someone's comfort, I expect, especially considering the size of her estate. So—"

She dug the little tablet from her pants pocket. "So she went to the hospital, where her death was just one of a series. She became the victim of a bizarre murderess—only, not the murderess everyone thought."

To Zelda she went on. "You visited Berenice often, and you knew the routines, including the medication routines. You were there earlier, I expect, before Berenice died—but after Jill Nash came on duty. Which means you could have slipped that vial into Jill's pocket."

Janet too was now staring narrowly at Zelda, who continued as expressionless as before. No further lights came from the driveway, nor any sounds.

"That was where things went wrong," Edwina went on, treading carefully now; too much truth might get her turned into dog food. "I'm not sure whose idea it was to get Carl working in the pharmacy, but once he was there he was supposed to do what he was told—be a good little worker, and wait."

Zelda's mouth was twitching with anger. "Probably someone made it worth his while, and promised to pay him even more," Edwina said. "Only he didn't just do what he was told, did he? He tried out the plan in advance on an old man named Walt Clemens, and then Millie Clemens began saying she'd seen how it happened."

"But," began Janet, "it was the same nurse, the one who—"

"Exactly," agreed Edwina. "Jill Nash was there, but only by coincidence. She'd been pulled from her usual ward. A most unfortunate coincidence for someone, as it turned out. Meanwhile, what mattered to Millie Clemens was her absolute belief that Jill Nash killed her husband—an idea which, if she kept insisting on it, was sooner or later going to be reinvestigated."

Edwina looked at Janet. "And there, of course, lay the rub. You see, Jill *didn't* put anything into Mr. Clemens's IV. All she did was turn it on. The potassium was already in it, put there unknowingly by an earlier medication nurse who thought she was dosing it with one of his legitimate drugs. Carl Wagner had switched the premixed solution that nurse gave with a mixture of his own devising, and if Millie were ever questioned carefully, professionally . . ."

"She might remember what she really saw?" Janet stopped, frowning as if working a difficult sum in her head. "Or what she didn't see. And then people might start figuring out . . ."

Edwina nodded. "That Walt Clemens *had* been murdered, and that it must have been planned in advance. But Jill didn't even know she would be working on the floor where Walt Clemens was a patient until just before she was sent there. She couldn't have done it. And once all those facts were understood, she would be a less attractive suspect in the other murders, because if someone *else* killed Walt Clemens . . ."

Come on, come on, she thought at the window, I'm getting to the good part. I'd prefer a more friendly audience.

"The letter," said Zelda slowly. "Carl must have heard us talking about it this afternoon. He must have gone and—"

"He went, all right," Edwina agreed, "because he knew if the Clemens case were reexamined it could sink him. Only not on his own. I think someone sent him, don't you? Possibly someone who had just realized how Millie Clemens could destroy a plan that had been in the works for months. A plan Carl had messed up."

Footsteps crunched in the gravel drive outside. "And now," said Edwina gratefully, "I think the police have arrived at last. How extremely helpful of them."

But no authoritative knock sounded; instead, as Edwina moved toward the front hall, the door swung open and Carl Wagner came in. "Hello, ladies. You all having yourselves a hen-party?"

"Fool," Zelda said, raising the little gun purposefully at him. But tin cans and varmints weren't quite the same as human beings; seeing her hesitation he crossed the room in three steps and grabbed the weapon from her hand.

"That's the trouble with women," he said unpleasantly, "they talk too much. Especially," he swung around to Edwina, "you."

"You *bastard*," Janet said tightly, "how *could* you—"

Glancing down, Zelda motioned minutely at the big dog still sitting unnoticed yet alert beside her chair.

"Grrmmph," Ruby agreed throatily, and charged.

NINE

RUBY'S massive forepaws smacked Carl in the chest, a hundred pounds of angry, determined dog startling him and then unbalancing him. His arms pinwheeled back as her teeth gnashed purposefully in his face; flailing as he fell he smacked his wrist hard on the corner of a rock-maple endtable.

The snap of the bone breaking came through clearly even to Edwina's ears, followed by his howl of fear and pain. The weapon sailed on impact from his hand, spun across the floor and came to rest against the kindling basket by the woodstove.

Quick as an eel, Janet sprang for it. Hurling herself the same way, Zelda stumbled and flung herself, scrambling on hands and knees. Meeting halfway to the prize the two women tangled, Zelda grabbing Janet's ankle and yanking on it while Janet tried beating away the older woman with frantic fists. Ruby had Carl Wagner straddled and was terrorizing him with truly wonderful effectiveness, her deep moaning growls predicting his imminent dismemberment should he so much as twitch an eyelid.

All of this took perhaps five loud, busy seconds; during them Edwina made her way thoughtfully among the inhabitants of Poole Farm to pluck up the little gun herself. Interestedly she inspected the weapon, noticing that it was loaded and in good repair. Then, experimentally, she fired the damned thing.

The shot clipped off the tip-tilted head of a porcelain figurine in the shape of a colonial drummer boy, perched by the window on a knick-knack shelf. After that the bullet punched a neat, round hole in the draperies and went on out through the glass with a sharp, satisfying *smack*.

Pleased, Edwina looked up. As she had intended, the sound of the gunshot combined with the sudden reek of cordite had concentrated everyone's attention marvelously. Janet and Zelda froze in mid-swat to gaze up at her in startled realization, Carl jerked involuntarily, his widened eyes rolling in his head, and even Ruby whimpered briefly, not releasing her prisoner.

"You didn't," said Edwina, "let me finish my story. But it wasn't a very good story anyway, was it? It left out one very important detail."

As she spoke, she noticed her own voice being drowned out by the ringing of an enormous gong, which in addition to its remarkable size seemed curiously to be located deep inside her head.

That gunshot, she realized; my ears. Even more interesting were sensations coming from her injured arm, as firing a pistol was apparently not on the list of activities recommend for healing it. Mentally she appended at least another year to the time she planned to spend howling in pain, assuming of course she ever got the chance to, and speaking of which where the hell was McIntyre? Luis, she thought, when I find you I am going to kill you, metaphorically and in several other long, drawn-out ways.

"Zelda," she said, "would you please call the police now? Any old police will be fine. I'd do it myself," she added, aiming the little gun at Janet, "but I'm kind of busy here."

"What are you *talking* about?" asked Janet plaintively. "I don't—you said *she* helped kill Aunt Berenice with *him*." She aimed a glare of hatred at the handyman.

Painfully, Zelda lifted herself off the floor; not looking at either Carl or Janet, she crossed to the chair by the telephone and sank into it.

Tears shone in the weathered creases of her cheeks. "No, she didn't say that. Finish your story, Miss Crusoe. All of it."

She emphasized these last words, which made Edwina hesitate. Surely the horrid facts didn't need to be spelled out completely, not to someone whom they could only hurt.

"She was my friend for forty years," Zelda said, seeming to understand this delicacy and discount it. "I thought when I first saw you she would have liked you, too. So tell me how she died. I know it's going to be awful and I'd much rather hear it from you. After that, I'll decide about the police."

"She's lying! Zelda, she's lying, don't believe her!" In Janet's eyes the fury of a trapped creature burned. "*Zelda—*"

Lie to her, whispered a voice in Edwina's ringing ear. She's old, she's tired, she doesn't need to know the worst. What good could it do her? Why give her more to suffer over?

She looked at Zelda, whose hands lay loosely in her lap. Crouched over Carl the dog glanced at her mistress, too, as if sensing those hands might command something new at any moment.

Indecisively Zelda eyed the telephone; perhaps, her look said, this was all some terrible misunderstanding, something they might yet clear up among themselves. Or, her perfect stillness warred against her sorrow, perhaps not.

Either way, the dog was the main thing now: it would do what she said, and it was big.

"Zelda," pleaded Janet. "Please listen to me. We can have it all back just the way it was before. We don't need the police. She's just trying to get us in trouble so she can help that nurse."

"Mrs. Bennington," said Edwina sadly, "was smothered."

As if in understanding, Ruby growled throatily. The young woman sprawled on the floor chewed her lip in calculation.

"She's lying, Zelda, she's—"

"What I kept having to ask myself," Edwina went on, speaking only to Zelda now, "was what the drug was for, if it wasn't to kill Mrs. Bennington. Because, you see, it did seem as if it had not killed her—according to the pathologist who examined her body, she really shouldn't have died from it."

She turned back to Janet. "It was meant to make the nurse look guilty. Carl dosed the heart-medicine vial with pancuronium and that was how the substance got into Berenice's tissues. That tainted vial was recovered from the wastebasket. The second vial Jill dropped into her pocket, where it could be found afterward at your insistence."

"In her pocket," Janet bit the words out. "You saw—"

"I saw," Edwina replied calmly, "your hands go into her pockets empty. You'd already switched the

188

vials, in the moments when Jill was busy manipulating the IV. She tossed the tainted Inderal vial into the trash, and set the other, the antibiotics vial that she meant to return to the pharmacy for billing purposes, on the bedside table. But Carl had supplied you with an empty pancuronium vial to use for the switch. That," she finished, "was why no antibiotics vial was ever found. At first I thought it must have gotten lost in all the confusion, but I suppose you took it with you and disposed of it somehow."

On the floor, Carl tried to protest. "Stay, Ruby," Zelda said, and Carl groaned helplessly. "Go on, Miss Crusoe."

"In the darkened room," Edwina said, "Jill didn't notice your movement, and she expected the vial she put down to be the one she picked up. She was stunned when she saw the label—but you weren't, were you, Janet? You visited often, you'd seen her do it all a dozen times. You knew just when to make the switch. The other two murders were to make it all look like a pattern."

Ruby shifted, whining, the desire to tear Carl's throat out plain in her pretty, tooth-studded grin.

"What," said Zelda, "about the smothering? I don't see—"

"Zelda, I *wouldn't*," Janet implored, "she's *lying*."

"As I said," explained Edwina, "the drug was never meant to kill her, only to muddy the waters and lay blame on Jill. Which left the killing itself still to be done, and there was just one weapon available."

She looked at Janet's hands, small but strong. "It only takes three minutes of oxygen starvation. You must have begun the moment Jill left the room, and she couldn't have fought hard. By the time the code team got there she was much farther gone than they realized, simply too far gone to bring back."

She shrugged. "The pressure from the resuscitation mask obliterated any marks you made with the pillows, I suppose."

Zelda rose from her chair. "Ruby, watch them," she commanded. The dog backed off Carl and sat at attention, waiting with perfect patience to see who Zelda wanted savaged next.

"She's a remarkable animal," Edwina said.

"Yes," said Zelda in a voice harsh with anger, "and she'll attack *anyone* on command, I guarantee. You'd better sit still."

She crossed the room, took the gun from Edwina's hand—the dog's gaze enforcing instant compliance with this—and hefted it expertly. "Now," she said, "I want to hear the truth."

Kneeling, she jabbed the small bright barrel at Carl's ear. Carl began to blubber. "It wasn't my idea, it was her, she said she'd get me fired if I didn't—"

"Carl," Janet uttered, "shut up."

Jab, jab. "If you didn't what?"

Carl sobbed, to no avail. "I'm an old woman," Zelda said, "and what's left of my life is spoiled, now. I would love to punish you for that. It would be worth whatever they can do to me to kill you, believe me. At least I could say I'd done that much, even if I didn't manage to stop you from killing Berenice."

Carl did believe, and so did Edwina. Zelda's voice was as chill and lifeless as a rattle of dead leaves; gazing at Carl she seemed to see through him into her own grave—or into his.

Between hitching sniffles he confirmed all Edwina had said. As he spoke, Janet tried once to get up, but at Zelda's gesture Ruby got to her feet, too, with eyes plainly purposeful, and Janet sat sullenly down again.

"So I tried a switch on the old guy," Carl finished, cradling his injured wrist resentfully. "How was I supposed to know the wife would be there, or the one nurse who I didn't want to be there, either? Hell, I wasn't going to do it for real without a run-through. It's not my fault things got screwed up."

"How long?" Edwina asked. "Had you been planning, I mean?"

"Two years," he replied tiredly, closing his eyes. "I knew Janet in Miami. She was just a skinny little whore who turned tricks for a meal and bed. She said we'd come up here an' score on her sick aunt, only it would take time. I came first, then her. What the hell." He turned his head away defeatedly. "I'm glad it's all over."

"Shut up," whispered Janet, "you stupid idiot, you shut your dumb big mouth—oh, hell, oh *hell*." She stopped, her jaw clenched thwartedly.

Just for a moment Edwina saw her as she must have been: big eyes staring out of a thin grimy face, all the cunning of a small, starved animal in her expression. And, thought Edwina, the moral complexity of an animal: eat or be eaten.

"You don't understand," the girl whispered. "She was nothing but a bossy old woman, always thinking she knew best. Do this, Janet; you should do that, Janet. If she sold the place now she wouldn't get ten cents on the dollar, but in ten more years—"

Carefully, Zelda raised the little gun and fired.

Janet screamed, slammed backward as if by a thrown punch; a splotch of blood blossomed on her shirtfront just below her shoulder. Carl yelled, scrabbling crabwise toward the hall as the dog leapt up again, barking wildly.

"Stay, Ruby." With calm deliberation, Zelda took practiced aim at Carl's head.

"Zelda!" Edwina jumped up. "Zelda, *don't*—"

In Zelda's eyes were the fear and pain, the awful loneliness of old age. "You," she said. "If you'd only stayed out of it, I would never have had to know all this."

Smiling faintly, she leveled the weapon. Its small dark eye stared into Edwina's own. Across the room, Janet whimpered.

Dry-mouthed, Edwina stared back. "Without the truth, you'd have stayed here with these two, until they killed you, too."

She held out her hand, ignoring the agony flaring in it. "It wasn't your fault she died, Zelda. You couldn't have saved her. There was no way you could have known. Besides, Berenice was your friend. She wouldn't blame you, would she? Don't spoil your memories of her now with pointless revenge."

Zelda paused. It seemed to take an age before she nodded brusquely once and dropped the gun into Edwina's keeping.

The thing weighed a ton; with an effort Edwina closed her fingers around the checkered grip.

"You'd better get the dog to find Carl," she said over the steady sound of Janet's weeping, "if he's still in the house. I'll watch the girl and telephone the police."

"That," said Martin McIntyre from the hallway, "isn't going to be necessary."

* * *

"I told you," said Harriet Crusoe, indulging pleasurably in her best-loved maternal prerogative, "that Clemens woman was the key to it."

Smiling over the teacups in the little parlor before the fire, her pen and notebook tucked into the chair beside her, she lifted a slice of nut bread from a silver tray.

"More bread, Mr. Ramirez?" she inquired, poising the silver server over his plate, and the cab driver nodded happily.

"Yes, Mother," Edwina replied, "but you didn't tell me *how* she was. Rather a significant omission, don't you agree?"

"Thank you, Mrs. Crusoe," said Luis Ramirez, trying hard to hide his astonishment and failing to; everywhere he looked some new marvel caught his eye. Even the tiny forget-me-nots on the china cups fascinated him; to distract himself he bit into the nut bread. "Delicious," he grinned through a mouthful.

"I'm glad you like it," said Harriet, pouring him more tea. "I'll ask the cook to send some home with you, for your family."

Luis, as it turned out, had not been able to get McIntyre on the telephone because McIntyre was interrogating Jill Nash. So, with a directness possible only in those to whom the worst has already happened, he had driven to the parking lot outside police headquarters, climbed onto the roof of the cab, and simply begun shouting for him.

This technique would have done little beyond getting Luis thrown into the slammer had McIntyre not heard his name being shouted so determinedly and come downstairs to see what all the commotion was, whereupon Luis gave him the ring and described how he had come by it.

Which, McIntyre had thought, sounded so much like the kind of thing only Edwina would do that he believed Luis at once and went where Luis said to go.

"Although," he said now from the small, upholstered settee where he perched uncomfortably, fearing with some justification that it might collapse under him at any moment, "I didn't know Luis would decide to follow, and I certainly didn't know my car would blow a headgasket on the way."

Fortunately, thought Edwina, since otherwise the Fiat would still be sitting in the Benningtons' woods. Once Carl and Janet had been dispatched, Luis had driven the Fiat here while she rode with McIntyre in the cab; just now her arm was barely able to shift across her lap, much less operate a standard transmission.

"The las' guy prob'ly didn't tighten it down so good," Luis theorized seriously about the headgasket. "I can fix tha' for you, though, you want. My frien', he's got a truck."

With a sigh, he gazed around again. "This is a very nice place you have here, Mrs. Crusoe. My wife, she would definitely love it."

"Thank you," Harriet told him again, bemused by the alien creature enjoying her nut bread. "But Mr. Ramirez, I am curious. What did you say to Mr. Wagner to make him stop, when he came running out past you from the Bennington house?"

Luis hesitated. "Actually I din' say nothing to him. What I did, see, I clipped him upside the head—" He clasped his hands together. "—like this. See, you don' need no gun for the close-up stuff. You hit a guy right, he's gonna drop jus' like you shot him, positively."

"I see," said Harriet, as if he had been explaining some exotic new method for the mulching of lawn shrubberies. "How very interesting."

She turned. "And where were you," she inquired

194

of McIntyre, "while my daughter was being menaced by large dogs and guns?"

"Now, Mother," began Edwina, "please don't start in on—"

But McIntyre only grinned. "I was hearing confessions. For which, by the way, I think I have you to thank."

Suspecting what was coming, Edwina repressed a smile while Luis looked curiously from Harriet to McIntyre and back again.

"Me?" asked Harriet, "but how could I—"

"Edwina had it all under control," McIntyre explained, "but the situation was unstable. If I'd burst in that front door, I think Zelda would have shot her, or the dog might have attacked someone. As it was, I entered by the kitchen door. That," he finished innocently, "is how the police are supposed to come in, isn't it?"

He helped himself to another piece of nut bread while Luis blinked uncomprehendingly. "What interests me," he went on, "is how Carl Wagner got hold of any morphine at all. That stuff is supposed to be locked up all the time, I thought."

Edwina swallowed a guffaw, washed it down with a sip of tea. "He must have had a key for the locked pharmacy bags, or got an impression of one somehow. I think he could use plaster of paris from the cast room for that."

"Oh, yeah," Luis put in knowledgeably, "tha's easy. You jus' make a negative, see, from whatever you got—wax, chewing gum, whatever, an' you make a positive from *that*, an'—"

He stopped, remembering that the man sitting next to him was a police officer. "Anyway," he finished unconvincingly, "I *hear* it's easy."

"Luckily," Edwina said, rescuing him, "I wasn't getting any premixed drugs, myself. The minute the pharmacy order sheets went downstairs and Carl read them, he knew I was there. That's also how he knew which patients were allergic to what—it's stamped on their drug orders. Too bad Millie wasn't so lucky."

"I checked," McIntyre said, "she's going to be okay."

"Oh," said Edwina, her pleasure at this news increased by the appearance of Maxie, trotting into the room with casual poise and leaping at once into her lap. "Hey, guy," she said, smiling in spite of the wicked throbbing in her arm, "feeling better?"

"You'll have to ask Watkins about that," Harriet said with an indulgent glance at McIntyre; wit, in her opinion, made up for almost any sin, and possibly even for the sin of not being to the manor born. "He gave him," she went on, "horse medicine, only a two-hundredth as much. I don't know of what."

Prutt, said the black cat, eyeing the cream pitcher. Edwina administered a few drops in a saucer. "But that's all," she warned him. "Rich diets don't agree with you."

"What I don' get, you don' mind I ask," said Luis, looking as if he thought a rich diet would agree with him very well if only he could manage to arrange one, "is how that guy Carl got that job he had. Don' you have to go to some kin' of school for that, something?"

"Not," answered Edwina, "to fill carts and push them. Which is all he was hired to do. All he needed was a few minutes alone once in a while, to switch the medications. He wasn't dumb, just uneducated—he read about the drugs in pharmacy textbooks, and Janet helped him pick the ones he would switch."

Harriet shared out the last few drops from the teapot. "The one I feel sorry for is Janet herself," she said, not sounding as if she felt sorry for her at all. "How horrified she must have been, Edwina, when you asked her to read you the letter."

"I suppose," said Edwina. "Realizing how it was all going wrong was bad enough, but finding out I was so close to the truth was worse. And she couldn't lie, because the letter would be surely asked for at Jill Nash's trial, as evidence, and then she would have to explain why it wasn't what she read to me."

She turned to McIntyre. "A trial, I assume, which has now been called off?"

McIntyre nodded. "I doubt Jill will be released tonight, but by tomorrow—you'll love her reason for running, by the way. It wasn't a letter from Mrs. Clemens at all. It was an itemized list from her father of what he'd spent defending her so far, plus a sermon on her rotten way of life, et cetera. Kind of blew away what little common sense she's got—she panicked, that's all."

"The man," said Edwina in exasperation, "has a cash register where his heart belongs."

Her watch read ten-thirty. "We'd better get back to the hospital—William Bell's going to have my head for taking off on him, and I have to have the IV put back in, too. Might as well get it done before the night shift." Sighing, she got up.

"Thank you for coming, dear," Harriet said, getting up too. "I confess I was a little concerned when I saw the report of the explosion on the TV news, especially when I couldn't reach you."

"Yes, Mother," said Edwina, smiling. "But you are right on our way home, after all, and I knew you'd be in a tizzy if I didn't present myself for inspection." She turned in a circle. "See? All parts present and intact." Then she winced. "Well, fairly intact. You'd better go on driving the Fiat, Luis."

Harriet's eyebrows went up. "Tizzy? Surely not. So nice to meet you, Mr. Ramirez, and thank you for all your help. You too, of course, Detective McIntyre."

Then, astonishingly for Harriet, she embraced him, leaving a faint smudge of face powder on his lapel.

"Martin, I mean. Such a fine old name. And in this house," she added, brushing proprietarily at bits of imaginary lint while ignoring the face powder, "of course from now on you must always use the front door."

McIntyre's lean dark face broke into a grin. "I'll take it as a compliment, Mrs. Crusoe. Come on, Maxie." He bent down for the cat who leapt into his arms cooperatively; even the richest of diets, it seemed, could not keep Maxie from missing his very own bed, toward which he now sensed he was heading.

Edwina missed her own bed, too, but comforted herself with the thought of the stiff dose of painkiller she would get at Chelsea Memorial, instead.

"Mrs. Crusoe," said Luis, wringing his small, neat hands anxiously together, "I hope you forgive me for asking this, but I'm a good driver, I can fix any kin' of machineries, an' I am a hard worker, too. An' with such a big place, here, I jus' wonder if maybe you might ever need—"

Harriet turned her head of elaborately arranged

silver-white hair very slowly toward Luis. Her face in the soft pink glow of the parlor was amused.

"You want a job," she said, "and you think I might give you one, is that it?"

Luis shifted unhappily from foot to foot. "Yeah, well. But tha's okay, Mrs. Crusoe, I guess you prob'ly don' got any—"

"Don't *have* any," she corrected briskly. "But as it happens I might. Watkins has some neighborhood boys part-time, but—"

She patted his shoulder. "Come back tomorrow, Mr. Ramirez, we'll talk about it. And I want to hear more about this business of copying keys, also. Just," she added judiciously, glancing at her pen and notebook, "the small details you've heard from other people, of course."

"Yes, ma'am," breathed Luis happily, "oh, yes, *ma'am*. And now," he announced ecstatically, "if you all excuse me, I gotta go an' hot-wire the sports car."

"Mother," said Edwina when Luis had gone, "do you really think it's wise to hire a cabdriver off the street? I mean he is terrific, of course, but Watkins might not enjoy the idea at all."

"I think Watkins will think it's a wonderful idea," Harriet replied, walking them to the front hall.

"For one thing it's my idea," she noted, "and for another that's how your father hired Watkins in London, forty years ago."

She looked past them into the chilly darkness. "Good night, dears," she said, pointedly including McIntyre in her farewell, and closed the door.

"How," asked McIntyre a few minutes later as he pulled the cab out onto the road, "did that happen?"

Edwina settled against him on the front seat, with

Maxie in her lap. The aching in her arm had receded a little, although she knew it would be back in all its ferociousness.

"With Mother? You're wearing her down by your persistence. You're good at persistence."

"Hmph," he said, "I guess I'm not wearing you down, though. You're as bullheaded as you ever were. You could have gotten killed out there today. Twice," he emphasized unhappily.

"Mmm. I know. Are you very angry with me?" In the glow of the dashboard she watched him gazing ahead. The road at this hour was nearly deserted; only the taillights of the little Fiat showed, pulling away rapidly.

"For the fright you gave me, yes." He frowned. "If I had my arm around you, though," he allowed, "I might be able to get over it faster. Seeing as you did come out all right."

Carefully, she shifted so that he could drape his arm about her. "I am sorry you were worried. Are you feeling better now?"

He glanced sideways. "A little. Rest your head on my shoulder, why don't you? There, much better. Now if you'll only say you'll marry me, I'll be fine. I do wish you would, Edwina, I suppose I'm old-fashioned to care, but—well. I just do," he repeated stubbornly, "wish you would."

Surprised, Edwina looked at him. It was not a subject they had ever discussed, but now it seemed he had been thinking about it on his own, worrying about it, wanting it. Thus she supposed she also might cautiously consider the idea.

As she did so she noticed that his coat smelled familiarly of cold fresh air and Old Spice aftershave, that his mere presence was easily the most effective painkiller she knew—much better than anything that came from a needle or a pill bottle, although perhaps also a good deal more addicting—and that he had not said a scolding word since she apologized for frightening him.

"You realize," she said slowly, "I am not normal marriage material. I'm too stubborn, too spoiled, and too opinionated."

"Yes," McIntyre agreed, his amusement audible, "you are."

"I'd have to keep my own apartment and my own work and all my own things and my own—"

"Self," McIntyre finished for her comfortably. "Yes, I do realize that, Edwina. It's why I'm wishing what I wish, you see. But for heaven's sake don't worry about it. There's no rush, and you don't have to do it at all if you don't want to. It's a wish, that's all, not a demand."

From her lap Maxie made a sound of contentment and was still again. City lights appeared in the distance, twinkling whitely. McIntyre snapped on the radio and salsa music came out: trumpets and guitars, a jubilant sound in the darkened cab.

"You should be careful what you wish for," she warned, "it might come true."

"That," said McIntyre, "is what I'm counting on."